In the Arms of a Rak

A DAMSEL BEYOND COMPARE

A Thrilling & Witty Historical Regency Romance Novel

In the Arms of a Rake Series

Emily Higgs

In the Arms of a Rake Series

In the Arms of a Rake Series

Copyright © 2024 Emily Higgs.

All rights reserved. No part of this book may be used or reproduced in any form whatsoever without written permission except in the case of brief quotations in critical articles or reviews.

This book is a work of fiction. Names, characters, businesses, organizations, places, events and incidents either are the product of the author's imagination or are used fictitiously. Any resemblance to actual persons, living or dead, events, or locales is entirely coincidental.

In the Arms of a Rake Series

In the Arms of a Rake Series

CONTENTS

Chapter One 7
Chapter Two 13
Chapter Three 19
Chapter Four 26
Chapter Five 32
Chapter Six 38
Chapter Seven 44
Chapter Eight 49
Chapter Nine 55
Chapter Ten 61
Chapter Eleven 67
Chapter Twelve 73
Chapter Thirteen 78
Chapter Fourteen 84
Chapter Fifteen 90
Chapter Sixteen 96
Chapter Seventeen 101

In the Arms of a Rake Series

Chapter Eighteen 107
Chapter Nineteen 113
Chapter Twenty 119
Chapter Twenty-one 125
Chapter Twenty-two 131
Chapter Twenty-three 137
Chapter Twenty-four 143
Chapter Twenty-five 149
Chapter Twenty-six 154
Chapter Twenty-seven 160
Chapter Twenty-eight 166
Chapter Twenty-nine 172
Chapter Thirty 179
Chapter Thirty-one 185
Chapter Thirty-two 192
Chapter Thirty-three 198
Author Note 204
About the Author 205

1

Chapter One

The stone edifice had stood for almost a century, forming and shattering many people's aspirations, observing the passage of time, and keeping an eye on the world as it changed outside of the turmoil that raged within. This was Cedric's second residence.

Since he was a youngster, he was attracted by the power that this site possessed, and he wished to sit on top of it with the magic wand in his hand. But now these stone walls were closing in on him, attempting to crush him, as they had done for countless others.

He was seated in front of the council, all of them gruffly elderly men staring at him as if he were an ordinary person whom they might dismiss in an instant. He recalled the first time he sat in front of the council in this manner; he was a strong Whitworth, and the men in front of him were delighted to have him on their side. He realized at that moment that he had equal power with them even before entering the party, and he resolved that the next time he sat here, he would be the one having control over them.

The reality was far different from his imagination. The look in their eyes plainly indicated that he was on thin ice, and he would need to be on his best defense if he wanted to save what was left of his dream.

"Lord Silvershire," The council chairman smiled as he said. It lacked emotional depth. He always enjoyed playing the deception game of breaking through someone's outer look and guessing what they actually felt within while not revealing one's own intention.

When he chose to become a politician, he learned the skill of making acceptable appearances at the right moments. Despite his reputation as a cold-hearted beast with a grim countenance that refused to be touched, he was empathetic and could pretty accurately predict a person's state of mind. It aided him in his play against his opponents, allowing him to exploit their weaknesses and cause them to lose control. He won disputes with a stone-cold impassive visage that never wavered, propelling him up the ranks of his party. It seemed evident that he would become the youngest president of any party in the parliament's history. He was recognized as a calm and level-headed politician.

But he was restless now, and it was becoming difficult for him to remain inactive while waiting for the verdict to be passed. This would have been the best day of his life, but it had been marred by the scandal that had put London into a rage. His elder brother, Percival, the future duke of one of Great Britain's oldest houses, has married a commoner, a lady whose mother had a more colorful background than the whole aristocracy put together.

Even though his family had welcomed them, he couldn't bring himself to accept their marriage, which threatened to destroy all he had worked for over the years. He wasn't sure whether he'd ever be able to forgive his brother and wife if his dream fell apart in this room right now.

Being a Whitworth has always been advantageous to his family. His brother played his cards well, threatening to halt the flow of money into the economy via their banks. The Crown Prince and his father supported him, ensuring his seat on the King's council. His mother utilized her status as King's cousin to demonstrate that they are still the most powerful family in the kingdom. His younger brothers were unaffected and seemed to embrace the mayhem.

His dream was the only one at stake. Even while the nobles were irritated by their display of power and the commoners were swayed by some type of fairy tale romance, none of them took a liking to a parliament member from the same family that sacrificed all to rescue their own.

They feared him, and his display of authority made many people uneasy, so they began to resist him. They didn't consider him one of them.

In the Arms of a Rake Series

Many people were horrified by his family's ability to affect public opinion and convert what had been a negative narrative about their daughter-in-law into something positive. He was a Prince who had everything.

"Lord Silvershire," the council leader remarked, "Many congratulations on your brother's wedding. I heard the ceremony was extremely spectacular."

"Thank you, Mr. Henry," Cedric said with a little grin. His committee chairman was not a member of the high nobility, and his mother's guest list did not include him. Curse his luck. Instead of neglecting and avoiding the wedding preparations, he could have given more attention.

"I hope you are aware of why the council has requested your presence," he went on to say.

"I'm afraid I'm not," Cedric said quietly. He knew he was meant to be the party's president, but he wasn't sure anymore. It was better to be safe.

"Well, we initially planned this meeting to bestow on you the Presidency of the party," Mr. Henry said plainly. "But."

He despised the man's foreboding silence. He was a major politician of his day. He was the third son of the baron of Dormer, making it impossible for him to ever obtain a noble title. He came to prominence as a political figure at a young age, serving as president of the liberal party for more than a decade before taking over as head of the council.

"Your older brother's scandal has had a significant impact on your standing. If we had to declare you President with elections on the horizon, the party would be vulnerable to assaults from the opposition. Instead of becoming powerful, we will become vulnerable. If the opposition plays this properly, the parliament may lose trust in us, making recovery harder. The best course of action will be to request your resignation," Mr. Henry added.

Cedric wasn't foolish; he knew this all along, but he hoped that given everything he had done for the party, they would place their trust in him and give him the opportunity to show that his Whitworth heritage would not influence the job he had done and would continue to do.

He remained mute, scared to open his lips and lose his calm.

"But we also understand your position as a Whitworth and considering all the hard work you had done for this party the committee has decided to offer you the Vice-Presidency," Mr. Henry went on to say.

Vice-presidency!! What total bullshit! They mocked him. He was the best candidate for President. But he didn't have any other alternative; he had to accept becoming someone else's shadow or quit the party totally.

He wasn't ready to quit after coming this far. He didn't appreciate being overstepped, but for the time being, he'll have to wait it out. Despite the failures, he swore to fulfill his ambition.

"I understand," Cedric responded, smiling, happy that he was still at the party and displaying true delight on his face. "I respect and accept the committee's decision. I pledge that this will not influence my loyalty to the party and that I will do my best for the greater good."

"Well, congrats; you made the proper decision. We will shortly announce the new President and Vice President. Thank you for your time, Lord Silvershire," Henry said, rising up and extending his hand for him to shake, signifying his dismissal. Cedric thanked everyone before exiting the committee meeting with a shattered dream and a wrecked reality.

2

Chapter Two

Cedric was boiling within. He was on his way to his office chamber when he came to a halt in front of the President's office. He couldn't believe he was that close to realizing his goal when it slipped from his grasp. As Vice President, he will have no substantial influence and will just serve as a show. It felt worse than being a party member.

He looked inside the office via the slightly open door. He has seen this hall several times. It was nothing extravagant; rather, it was extremely modest, with little adornment, yet it always seemed like a jewel on his crown.

"My Lord," someone greeted him, jolting him back to reality.

"Yes," he said.

In the Arms of a Rake Series

"Lord Vernon is asking of you in his office, my Lord," The youngster spoke. Cedric groaned, striving to expel the hatred inside him, and followed the child to Lord Vernon's office. Lord Vernon was one of five council members, along with Mr. Henry. He never liked him and had previously disregarded him completely. But given his current position, he had to sacrifice his pride.

The youngster knocked on the door and entered before him to announce his arrival.

"Lord Silvershire," Lord Vernon responded, feigning excitement. He was a superior, and Cedric was meant to bow to show respect, but their stations in society varied since Cedric was the Duke of Silvershire. Lord Vernon was Earl of Eldon, and he'd be damned if he ever bowed to this man.

"Whiskey?" Lord Vernon asked.

"No, thank you," Cedric said curtly, but Lord Vernon seemed unaffected.

"Well, I must say it was quite unfortunate for you to lose the Presidency of the party," he remarked, drinking his whiskey and returning his expression to normal. Cedric balled his fists. He was seldom aggressive, but everyone was getting on his nerves today.

"It is unfortunate," Cedric said, emphasizing each syllable.

"A man of your skill and determination, I am convinced you will be the next President," Lord Vernon replied, "But it may take a lot longer than you'd expect, don't you think, Lord Silvershire? I mean, the future President will only be picked when the present one retires or something awful occurs to them." Lord Vernon smiled at his own awful joke. Cedric stood rigidly.

Cedric recognized this man's willingness to get things done by hook or crook. While this was the way of the world, he never intended to do serious harm to anybody. "Whether we win the Presidency or not, the work we all perform for the party will not be diminished. In the end, we're all here to serve," Cedric said quietly.

"Indeed," the Lord said, "But the glory always goes to the one sitting on the throne and everything else is insignificant and expendable."

"Fortunately, none of us will ever sit on The Throne," Cedric replied arrogantly from the sofa, daring Lord Vernon to continue the argument.

"But one can sit in front of the throne with the same power," Lord Vernon said with an ugly grin.

"What do you mean?" Cedric inquired, perplexed; it couldn't be what he suspected.

"There is no restriction that only the party President may be selected as Prime Minister. The council can sway the decision and nominate anyone as Prime Minister for the next term, even if the President remains the same," Lord Vernon cleverly said.

Of course, it was feasible. He recalled Lord Vernon as the Liberal Party's Prime Minister contender, despite the fact that he was not the President. Unfortunately, they lost the election. Lord Vernon seemed to be ready to assist him along the same road, but he must have something in return, for nothing comes for free.

He was very conscious of the Whitworth blood rushing through him, which had provided him with this chance. The scandal had merely dented Whitworth's reputation, and with the royal family's unwavering backing, they remained above everyone else.

"That could happen," Cedric said cautiously. He did not want to come out and ask Lord Cardwell how to accomplish it. He has to be cautious with this one.

"I really believe in you, Cedric," Lord Vernon stated, making Cedric grimace as he said his name nonchalantly. "I believe you are more than capable of not just controlling this party, but also this nation. If it weren't for the recent scandal." Lord Vernon's demeanor conveyed guilt, but there was also a sense of contentment as if he was pleased with the outcome.

"I appreciate you, Lord, for believing in me, and I think there is a way I can work for it. After all, the scandal's fire will soon dissipate," Cedric remarked with phony respect, keeping a close eye on him. He'd given the other an opportunity; now he'd wait and see.

"Of course," Lord Vernon responded, gulping the remainder of his whiskey. "The first step will be to correct your brother's mistake."

"I am afraid I do not understand, my Lord," Cedric said. He was not going to listen to a stranger prying into his family members' lives. Even if he wasn't pleased with Percival, Percival had been tremendously joyful, and he would not allow anybody to jeopardize his brother's marriage. It was completely unacceptable.

"Whitworth always married into a noble family, your brother strayed from his path but you are also the son of the Duke of Whitworth, second son but Duke nonetheless," remarked the Earl of Vernon. "And the first step to achieving your dream will be restoring the glory of Whitworth as it once was by marrying a highborn lady from a noble family," He proceeded complacently. "A good marriage is always a strength in any political endeavour."

Cedric examined Lord Cardwell's words. He was never interested in marrying. When he chose to become a politician, he realized he would never have time to play with his family, so he dismissed the idea entirely.

"Well, there will be no more parliament negotiations. My wife has been very concerned about it. All ladies want to speak about are gorgeous costumes and balls, such simple animals," Lord Vernon sighed, "Will you be an attendant at tonight's dance, my Lord?"

No! He was not attending the ball. He had better things to do. He had previously attended several balls for the purpose of his brother's nuptials. No one suspected Whitworth's second son was opposed to his family's recent wedding, and he intended to keep it that way. But now, Lord Vernon has stated it.

"Yes, my Lord," Cedric said calmly.

"I have to go immediately. We'll meet at the ball, Lord Silvershire," Lord Vernon replied. Cedric rose up and exited the room, putting together the discussion and reading between the lines. Lord Vernon was not a charitable man; to him, everything was business.

If he was willing to assist Cedric, it is likely that he expected something in return. And he could really know what it was.

Cedric was well-dressed for the gala. He wasn't the most attractive of his brothers, and he wanted it that way, but today he had a mission to begin the first step toward putting things in order. And he knew just who was going to help him realize his aspirations.

As soon as he arrived, he approached Lord Vernon. "Lord Vernon," Cedric tilted his head slightly, a ghostly grin on his lips, "I hope you are enjoying the ball."

"Lord Silvershire," Lord Vernon said eagerly, "It is a pleasure to meet you outside those stone walls. Please allow me to introduce you to my wife and daughter." Both women curtsied to Cedric. He invited Miss Vernon to dance and gave her a soft kiss on the back of her hand while looking at her. She was supposed to be his passport to living his dream.

3

Chapter Three

Cedric awoke with the sense of a fresh beginning. The ball had been a success, and despite his stone-cold demeanor, which kept the women at a distance, he was certain he had enchanted Lady Vernon. Now all he had to do was keep up the charade and stand at the altar with her.

Lord Vernon had made it clear that he wanted Cedric to marry his daughter, and given how his daughter had swooned at his sight, everything else was relatively simple. He awoke with a bright grin, which was unusual for the folks on his estate. Everyone refrained from pausing to stare at their master, who seemed more attractive than ever.

His footman made him tea and brought him the daily Ledger. He didn't want to ruin his mood by reading Ledger's lame attempts to tarnish his family's reputation and save their face.

In the Arms of a Rake Series

His butler informed him that his younger brothers Octavian and Dominic had paid him a visit. His family had retreated to their country house for the summer to escape the heat of the scandal, but he had steadfastly remained in London. So, it was surprising that his brothers were on his estate. When he entered the parlour to see his brothers, he saw them speaking with his father, while his mother instructed his butler to make lunch for everyone. He couldn't believe his relatives organized a revolution and took over his land without his knowledge. He should locate another estate that none of his family members will be aware of.

He welcomed everyone, and his mother chastised him and his younger brother for not visiting them often enough, while his father merely grinned at himself. As they sat in the parlour, it was clear that his parents were overjoyed to have all of their children back together. Octavian and Dominic spoke as usual, and everything was well at his house until his elder brother and wife joined them for lunch. How he despised the awkward stillness! Everyone was aware of his attitude toward their marriage, and the discomfort only grew.

"Cedric," Percival was the first to speak out. "How are you? How is Parliament?"

"I am doing fine. The parliament voted not to elect me as the party's President. The Whitworth controversy has just recently subsided, and it has the potential to damage the party," Cedric said bluntly. He was never one for sugarcoated remarks, and he wanted them to feel regret.

"It is their loss," Octavian remarked, chewing on his muffin. "They should know better than that."

"There must be a way, Cedric. I know your brain has already begun working on the approach," Dominic said.

"Indeed," he said, "I am going to marry Lady Vernon, daughter of the Earl of Vernon."

"What!" Dom, Tavi, and his father all sputtered simultaneously. "How will getting married get you the Presidency?" His mom was perplexed.

"Marrying the Earl's daughter, who is a member of the council, will undoubtedly clear my path to success," Cedric said, undisturbed by everyone's looks. It was a subtle jab at his brother, who married a lady below his class and was shunned by society.

"Listen, Cedric Whitworth; you will not marry for political benefit. I will not allow it," his mother said.

"Think about it, son: what if Lord Vernon finds out? How will Lady Vernon react if she discovers you married her for selfish reasons?" His father inquired.

"Lord Vernon was the one who suggested it, father. Lady Vernon recognizes her position and authority after marrying the Whitworth and has no objections to the arrangement. I believe both father and daughter are working together to get me married," he remarked gently.

"Even a stronger reason why you shouldn't marry her, brother," Dom remarked worriedly.

"I think Cedric understands what he is doing Dom," he added. Tavi was never the person closest to him, but he was always there to encourage him.

"Indeed," Percival said, "He has always been the wisest of us all. And I have trust in him to make the correct judgments." Cedric was stunned by his elder brother's statements. He never expected any of them to understand.

"Thank you, brothers," Cedric said. His parents were not pleased with him, but they had always given their children the opportunity to make their own decisions, had trust in each of them, and had the authority to protect them all if anything went wrong. Nothing could persuade him to alter his decision, so everyone returned to their meal.

"How are you, my Lady?" Cedric asked Hannah, stunning not just her but everyone else at the dinner.

"I am well, my Lord, thank you," Hannah responded simply, still closed off to him, and he couldn't blame her; he hadn't felt compelled to make a good impression on her.

"You look different somehow," Cedric added, "I take it that my brother is treating you well."

Cedric was concerned about the influence her choice to remain with her brother had on his career, but being here surrounded by his family made him feel at ease. In his heart, he knew he shouldn't blame her or his older brother, but he'd need time and space to accept the situation as is.

"Of course, I am treating her well," Percival bragged.

"Would you like some wine?" Cedric murmured, disregarding Percival, when he observed she just had a glass of water.

"Uh, no, my Lord, thank you," Hannah said, glancing at Percival. A wordless discussion passed between them; they were much like his parents, and the hatred in his heart eased somewhat. His family was supposed to return to the mansion after lunch, but instead, they had made themselves at home in the parlour. While his oldest brother and wife spoke with his mother, his father and younger brother seemed to have launched a race to empty his cellars.

Cedric coughed, catching everyone's attention.

"Pardon me, I have some work and would be immensely grateful if all of you gave me some privacy and peace," he added with an annoying grin on his lips.

"How can you throw us out when you have invited us for the luncheon?" Dom inquired with a raised eyebrow.

"I did not do such things. You all came here uninvited," Cedric denied

"Now, now, it was me who planned this," His mother said, "Percival had asked the family to assemble, and knowing Cedric, I thought going over unannounced would be the best course of action. Now, Percival sweetheart, let's finish this before Cedric busts a vein.

"Thank you, Mother," Percival rose up, beaming warmly. "Thank you, everyone, for coming on such short notice."

Cedric met his teeth. He didn't even get the notification, yet it was his house.

"We wanted everyone together to share the news with you," Percival remarked enthusiastically as he got up and raised his wine glass.

"What are you doing?" Hannah inquired, bewildered by her husband, which caused Cedric to laugh.

"Making an announcement," Percival said dumbly, as Hannah moaned and covered her face behind her palm. "Oh, Brother!"

"What? What's the announcement?" Dom inquired enthusiastically.

"Well, Hannah and I are going to be parents," he said triumphantly, causing everyone to shout with excitement. The situation was chaotic. When Dom and Tavi began bickering about who would be the godfather, Cedric resisted the desire to box them. He also congratulated the couple.

"My Lord," their butler said to Cedric as everyone celebrated the news.

"Yes," he answered, without turning away from his demented family. His parents seemed to be already aware. Only the brothers were aware of the news.

"I hate to interrupt, my Lord, but there is a child outside who is demanding an audience with you and refuses to go until he sees you. He said he works in parliament," his butler informed.

"Very well, bring him to my office," Cedric instructed.

He had to force his family to go since they were unwilling to stop celebrating. He said goodbye to everyone and made his way to the workplace. He entered his office and paused at the doorway when he saw a lady in a tailcoat and slacks, her glossy ginger hair cascading down her back, inspecting the paperwork on his table.

The lady must have detected his presence and turned around before he could summon his guards. This was an unsettling scenario that needed to be handled carefully.

"Who are you?" Cedric inquired calmly. Her lovely topaz eyes stared at him, and her ginger hair streamed behind her. She resembled an intriguing warrior.

"I am Evelina Winchester."

4

Chapter Four

"I am Evelina Winchester," she answered, gazing at him. "And you are going to pay for what you have done," she said, stunning him.

"Evelina Winchester, as in Lady Evelina Winchester, daughter of Earl of Winchester the leader of the conservative party," he added with a look of confusion.

"The one and only," she said. What in God's name was happening today? First, his family showed there unannounced, and now this lady threatens him on his estate. He needed to discover another estate that no one knew about.

"My Lady, what can I do for you?" Cedric inquired, attempting to keep his voice down.

She moved angrily towards him, forcing him to take a step back. She paused in front of him, jabbing her finger into his chest. She was closer than society indicates an unmarried man and woman should be to one other, which made him uneasy.

"How dare you? How can you stoop that low?" She replied. She was furious, and her ginger hair made her appear even more evil.

"Perhaps we can sit down and discuss what I have done my Lady," he murmured, a little terrified of the woman in front of him.

He is familiar with Evelina Winchester, the only daughter of the Conservative Party's leader. She made her debut in society two years ago, and despite her parents' strict views, she has remained unmarried to this day.

He'd seen her at countless balls and heard a lot about her from the guys who courted her, as well as those who tried but failed. They all wanted to marry her for her dowry since she was not a typical beauty.

He had never paid attention to her, but she was a laughingstock. Men had always spoken about her or rather mocked her.

She was taller than the majority of the ladies and lacked flesh in some areas, making her seem even taller. When she stood in front of him, she reached up to his chin, her furious topaz eyes staring into him. Her face was often caked with too much powder, which combined with her ginger hair gave her a ghostly appearance.

She tried too hard, causing a man to lose interest. But her money alone should have made a wise man turn a blind eye to everything unfavorable.

Nonetheless, she remained without a proposal, and he now knew why. She was angry and stupid. Entering an estate of her father's adversary in such a disguise. She may be damaged in such a manner that her father would be unable to hold his head high.

"Do not think you will be able to let go so easily, my Lord," she whispered, edging away from him.

"I am afraid you are in the wrong estate, my Lady," He continued, his patience dwindling, "I am Lord Cedric Whitworth, Duke of Silvershire. I am from the Liberal Party, while your father is the leader of the Conservative Party."

She narrowed her eyes at him, her rage becoming even stronger. Cedric wasn't sure whether it was because she was at the wrong estate or because she was in the proper place and he had insulted her intellect by treating her like a child.

"I can't believe this. You are more of a rotten bastard than I thought," she said angrily. Cedric was surprised by her remarks. Her father was a conservative icon, and his daughter was spouting stuff that no woman should hear.

"I beg your pardon," he said, surprised.

"Oh, don't you play innocent after what you have done," she cried, crossing her arms. His head had begun to hurt.

"My lady, pray to tell me what have I done?" He expressed irritation.

"Are we playing coy? Perhaps I should throw the ledger at your face to refresh your memory," she remarked, returning her gaze to his table.

One day, he didn't read a ledger, and it invited this insane lady to his home. He moved to the wine decanter, where the ledger was resting on its side. When he opened the first page, he was surprised to see her father.

Lady Winchester was found in Duke Wayton's library reading the prohibited book "A Modern Proposal to Women by Anonymous".

Lord Winchester had always had conventional beliefs and morals, and while lecturing about their significance, he failed to instill them in his daughter. The daughter who had failed to marry in the previous two seasons was discovered reading a controversial book in the library rather than attending the ball. He knew why she was furious, but why was she upset with him?

"This is sad, but I can promise you that it has nothing to do with me. I believe you should find the person who caught you in the library, my Lady," he replied dismissively.

"I did. It's you," she said.

"And where in the world did you get that idea?" He replied, gazing at her aggressively. She should have fled his home in terror, but instead, she seemed to be prepared for combat.

"There was only one man who saw me reading in the library and he told me he was there to meet you," She said, "He was your man, wasn't he?"

"You trusted him because he mentioned my name. Are you crazy?" Cedric stated. He lifted his palm in front of her, stopping her before she could say anything: "And even if that was the case, there is no proof that I was behind this."

"But you had the motivation," she said. He couldn't imagine he could be much more upset.

"Everyone is aware that you lost your position as President of your party," she said plainly, "And it is evident you needed something to make up with the council. So, you mocked the opposition leader's daughter, knowing full well that it would tarnish their image while giving you an edge among your peers. "How low can you get?"

Cedric couldn't help but marvel at the woman's boldness. She was making charges without evidence against her father's opponent in his own house. And who was this man who was attempting to get him involved with the enemy?

"How do you know this? It has not been announced yet. Or, better still, how do you know about the opposing party's internal affairs? Cedric inquired suspiciously.

"A secret is never a secret in the political world, my Lord," she said angrily.

"And not everything you hear is true, my Lady," he said, reflecting her displeasure.

Cedric took a big breath. He couldn't allow this obnoxious lady to get under his skin. It was time he sent her home.

"My lady," Cedric responded gently, "I'm sorry the man lied to you about my participation in such a horrible incident. I may have lost the

Presidency to the party, but this does not imply I have lost my skill or work ethic. I'm not foolish enough to damage an innocent woman's reputation, which may ruin all I've fought for, and it's honestly beneath me.

Now, if you'll excuse me, I have business to attend to." Cedric dismissed her, expecting her to depart, but she lingered there staring at him, which he reciprocated.

"It is getting late, my lady," He said. "You should leave." When he refused to back down, she put her hair back into her cap and shut the door behind her. "I will not let you get away with this," she said before departing. He was already fatigued, and the day hadn't even ended yet.

5

Chapter Five

Evelina was infuriated. She kept reflecting on her interaction with Cedric Whitworth. He was a horrible bastard. She couldn't believe he would lie to her face. She was not an idiot; she saw that he would profit the most from assaulting her father.

"Evy, Evy," She heard her mother call her, "Are you sick? Why are you clutching the fork like you want to murder someone with it?"

"I am sorry, Mother," Evelina relaxed, glancing over at her father, who had ceased looking at her when the ledger reported on her library incident. He was disappointed in her, and her determination to make Cedric Whitworth pay became even stronger.

All night, she pondered how to get him to admit he was guilty and then publicly apologize. When the morning arrived and she was well-rested, her wrath had faded, and she began to reflect on all that had happened between them. He had a point when he suggested he'd be in much greater danger if anybody discovered he was behind it all.

But desperation may make a man lose his wits, and she was not going to give up until she found out who was behind this. If Cedric Whitworth was as innocent as he claimed, someone was attempting to harm his reputation, or it may be a hoax. He may have ordered his lackey to reveal his identity in order to demonstrate how ignorant he is, or he could be speaking the truth.

Whatever it was, whoever did it, she was determined to get to the bottom of it, and she was willing to become a friend or adversary of Cedric Whitworth. She wore another of her tailcoats. Her slim stature allowed her to disguise herself in men's attire, and her father's large hat concealed her ginger hair. She must use caution while speaking or addressing another person. She couldn't believe she had to wear such clothing to meet Cedric Whitworth.

She'd seen him at different balls since she made her debut, and he always seemed to be a fearsome figure that everyone feared. He possessed an extremely chilly demeanor that captivated Evelina. She wanted to poke him to see whether he really had flesh or if he was always composed of stone. She wondered whether she could elicit any emotion from his stern expression.

From a young age, she knew that no one is your friend in the political sphere, and she avoided both her father's friends and foes, including him. She had promised her mother that she would spend the day with her friend Portia, yet here she was early in the morning spying on Cedric Whitworth's estate. In her wrath, she took the unwise decision to enter his estate. He could have done anything to her, but he chose to let her go since she was not going to push his boundaries. She was waiting for him to leave his estate so she could accompany him to his office chamber in the parliament building.

She paid the driver lavishly when she arrived at parliament. She was relieved that it was the correct carriage and that he had gotten down in parliament. Evelina intended to follow him quietly, but his long legs and velocity forced her to race after him. Some of the guys stared at her suspiciously but did not dare to stop her. She cursed Cedric once again. She had nearly come up to him when the guard stopped her and looked at her suspiciously.

"Name and purpose," he continued, presenting a registration to her. She filled in the information with her right hand, making it as incoherent and acceptable as possible. She tipped her hat and hurried off to locate Cedric. He was nowhere to be located.

It was her first time in her father's office. Her father never spoke about his job. He thought that politics was not for women and that the strain may be too severe. It must be true, and her rage grew as she realized she had to be there for this terrible man. Evelina walked from room to chamber, hoping to locate Cedric, until she glimpsed him through a door seated, and stormed in without hesitation.

"There you are," she said, realizing that not only him, but three other guys were staring at her in disbelief.

"And who you might be?" One of them asked.

"Apologies, my Lords," Cedric rose up and walked towards her, frowning. He stood alongside her, grasping her arms firmly. "Please pardon him."

"Who is he?" He seemed to be rather young; how did he enter the building?"

"He just began training for footman at my estate and has no manners, so please forgive us. We'll postpone our meeting for now," Cedric said, dragging her out of the rooms.

"I am sorry," she muttered, as his grip on her arms tightened and began to pain her. She had made him furious, and it was better to remain silent for the time being. She strained to see where he was bringing her, and to her horror, she spotted her father approaching them. No one else knew her, but she was certain that her father would, and who knows what would happen to her. She needed to think quickly. She could not allow Cedric to drag her in front of her father.

Her brain stopped at the point of imminent danger, and she saw her father conversing with one of his colleagues as they moved right towards them. She couldn't take her gaze away, and before her father could pass them, she was grabbed and hunched in a dark part of the building. She glanced up to discover that she was pushed against Cedric Whitworth, with just a hairbreadth of room between them. His ebony eyes were frighteningly malevolent, and his minty breath fanned her cheeks.

She pulled backward away from him, but there was very little room left. She opened her lips to complain, and he quickly clamped his hands over her mouth, indicating her to be silent. A quiver of excitement raced through her. It reminded her of the adventure stories she'd read about bold knights. She had always wanted to be a knight, but the reality was just the contrary; she was not the knight, and this disgusting man was protecting her from her father.

She pushed Cedric's fingers away from her lips and remained silent, pouting at the turn of events. He took a cautious glance outside and motioned for her to follow him, and she did so quietly, glancing around carefully.

When she entered his room and closed the door behind them, she exhaled deeply. She glanced up to see Cedric Whitworth looking enraged, his ebony eyes burning with fire.

"Need I even ask, my Lady?" He emphasized her unladylike behavior, ridiculing her at every point.

"I thought about what you said," she said, simply raising his brows. He was always a man of few words: "Someone had attempted to smear my reputation, and it may be you. However, if it has nothing to do with you, someone is also attempting to harm your reputation. And I need to locate that person."

"Why?" He came perilously near to losing his cool.

"Whoever they might be, they will pay for dragging my reputation through the mud and you will help me discover them," she replied with a smile.

"No, I will not," Cedric responded firmly.

"Why not? Don't you want to know who is attempting to use your name in this?" She asked, confused.

"No one would dare use a Whitworth name so callously," he added. "It was only because of you that they had the audacity to drag me into this."

"So, why is that? Why just me?" She inquired, puzzled.

"Because you are foolish."

6

Chapter Six

"Because you are foolish," he said plainly.

"You bastard," Evelina said, her rage rising. "How dare you call me foolish?!"

Cedric remained quiet, his expression indicating that she should reflect on what she had been doing up to this point. Regardless of what he believes, she was not being silly; she may have been a fool, but what else could she do? Sitting and doing nothing was never her style. But he wouldn't understand, given his position and authority. If she wanted Cedric Whitworth to assist her, she needed to remain calm.

"It is very ungentlemanly of you to say that a woman is foolish," she remarked with gritted teeth.

"Everything you have done till now is very unladylike, so it doesn't matter," said he.

"I'm not stupid. I know what I'm doing," she murmured, turning away from him with a childish pout.

"What you are doing is wrong!" he said.

She ignored him and wandered about his office, his gaze following her every movement. This was becoming crazy.

"What are you doing?" He inquired, agitated.

"Trying to find the clues," she said casually.

"My lady, do you really think I would leave clues this easy for you to find out," he responded without hesitation. Why was he keeping up with her?

"I have to try," she murmured, glancing around.

"My Lady, please think about this carefully," he added quietly. "You were certain I was the one behind this the day before, and now you want my aid to find out who did it. How can you trust me so easily?"

"I do not," she answered, rising up. "I do not trust you, Lord. I know better than that, but do I have a choice? I don't know where to start, and the fact that you haven't thrown me out or reported me to my father is enough for me to continue ahead since others won't even listen to me."

He didn't understand her motives and didn't want anything to do with her, but a flash of vulnerability in her eyes as she delivered the last words piqued his curiosity.

"What are you going to do once you catch that person? How will you get them to pay?" He asked.

"I don't know," she responded after a little quiet.

"My Lady, it would be better if you forgot about this whole situation. The ton will quickly forget, and when there is another controversy, they will stop talking about it altogether. We don't need to lose sleep over such trivial matters," he stated gently.

"It might be frivolous for you, my Lord, but I am sick of everyone ridiculing me," She said frustrated. "Every time someone raises crazy rumors about me, and this time Ledger went too far by publishing them in order to reach my father. Every time someone notes that I am still single, my father becomes a little more upset with me."

"I need to ask you whether the rumor is genuine. Because it is a very lame one," he said.

"Why does it matter? What I read in the library is of no concern to anyone," she said.

Cedric found it surprising. He had never liked her parents or the circles they moved in. They were such traditionalists, and her parents had particularly objected to his brother's choice of wife. He assumed that since their daughter was discovered with such an iconic book, they must have kept her trapped within a tower.

"You have to consider all the possibilities, my Lady," he replied. "Starting with I might be the one that could be behind this..."

She laughed, causing him to stop speaking.

"If that is true, you are awfully bad at it," she replied, laughing. The only thing on Cedric's mind was getting her out of his office. If anybody recognized her, he would be doomed.

"We need a plan," she said after a minute of thought.

"I have better things to do," Cedric dismisses her. "Please see yourself out."

Evelina was more obstinate than Cedric could have imagined, but she had no idea how stubborn he was himself. So, when she sat in front of him, confronting him, he ignored her. Evelina was growing upset since he was behaving as if she wasn't in his office. She was becoming impatient. They must have sat in quiet for a long time before her gaze fixed on his and he just continued working. A young unmarried lady was defenseless, and he was like a rock.

"Are you impotent?" She thought aloud. Cedric turned to her with a deadly stare. Definitely not the stone; he looked like the devil incarnate. She sprang up and went without looking back. Her foolish ego had placed herself at a disadvantage once again. She should be more elegant like a woman, but she has never been good at it. She should be glad that he was a true gentleman, although sometimes ran his mouth too much. He never made a move on her. It's no wonder that she had never met a man who considered her attractive.

She was annoyed that her journey had to stop today. She had to return to the estate, where her mistress was waiting to instruct her how to be more ladylike. It was humiliating; she should have been married by now, with a child or two, like all the other ladies her age, with the exception of those who choose to remain single. She never wanted to live her life alone. She wanted to be loved and marry a wonderful man, but she had no idea there were so few good men. All others who courted her simply tolerated her because of her dowry, and they either gave up or attempted to subdue her. She felt happy being true to herself.

It was a comfort that her parents never pressured her to marry, but even if they didn't say it to her directly as their only child, she could feel their joy when men expressed interest in her. And mask their sadness when the man rejects her or she pushes him away. Her mistress has always instructed her to conceal her actual identity and behave as the man in front of her wishes. Her mistress has always told her to be glad that she was born into a wealthy family and that her dowry was enough to get men to notice her even if she was unattractive.

She had one less thing to be concerned about with Cedric Whitworth. The father and his brothers, who were always surrounded by the most gorgeous ladies, would never show any interest in her. But she should be cautious with her emotions, for Cedric Whitworth was a gorgeous man. His black eyes complemented his dark hair, and his confident attitude with the elegance of a real ruler set him out even more. The deity must send the most beautiful of his angels since no one else is worthy to stand at his side.

Evelina waited anxiously to meet Cedric Whitworth again. She knew she could trust him and relied on him since he had warned her about himself several times, never hurt her, and protected her from her father. She needed to make a plan. It's always possible that he was behind it, but until she confronts him, she'll never know. She was terrible at planning and would usually do whatever she felt like at the time. This was going to be challenging, but she was never one to give up.

In the Arms of a Rake Series

7

Chapter Seven

Cedric could finally breathe freely. He has been on alert for the last several days. After Lady Evelina Winchester ambushed him in his office only days after barging into his estate, he was always on guard. He was relieved that no one had observed them together and started any unpleasant rumors.

He was relieved ton had forgotten her blunders so soon, for he knew the damage her reputation would endure. Previously, he would disregard rumors and scandals in society since he was at the top of the ladder, unreachable by everyone. However, having gone through it with his own family, he would not wish it on anybody else.

He found it difficult to accept the embarrassment that any scandal brings to a highly respected family, as well as the stain that would remain on their reputation indefinitely.

It seems that she had finally given up on her misguided quest. She had unwittingly warned him about the shadows lying in the darkness, ready to rear their heads now that he was weak. Someone was attempting to harm his reputation by giving her the idea that he was behind it. What an absurd and sad act! He never did anything halfheartedly. If he wished to tarnish her reputation, her family would have been shunned by the ton.

She was naive and fanciful, endangering herself and everyone around her. It's amazing she wasn't involved in a major controversy; even the rumors circulating about her were insignificant. Her father certainly had a lot on his plate with a child like her.

The cynical side of him urged him to be wary not just of the ones attempting to capture him, but also of her. This might all be part of her father's complex scheme to bring down not just him, but his whole party. After all, since joining the liberal party, he has publicly and steadfastly opposed him and won several debates.

The timing of his entrance into his life was perfect, as he was attempting to rescue the last of Whitworth's reputation after losing the Presidency and being pushed into the shadows. She might be waiting for the right moment to attack. He wishes she would return to her regular life so that he may resume his.

His family had returned to London after spending the summer in the countryside, away from the roaring flames of the Whitworth affair. Everything would never be the same again, but he was adjusting and figuring out how to go on. After a rough year, there was finally serenity and a new life will soon begin in their family. He was looking forward to his brother's child's arrival in this world. He also intended to marry Lady Vernon this year. The courtship had dragged on for too long. He wanted to get it over with soon since it was quite obvious what both sides wanted from this relationship.

He had always attended balls and soirees to signal his presence, but now he had to remain for hours performing stupid dances when he might have spent his time doing something more productive. He needed to make plans to propose to Lady Vernon before the season ended, but she had been acting strangely recently. It has delayed his marriage proposal. Lady Vernon never said that she was opposed to the marriage or that her father pushed it on her. He realized she was doing this for the benefit of her father; after all, she was only a pawn in men's games.

They will not have a loving marriage because it is just impossible. He intends to fulfill his responsibilities to the best of his ability, but, like her father, his goal is more important to him than playing family. Life would be easy with her, after all, her father was a politician, and she would make an excellent bride to another politician, knowing all of the hazards involved, unlike someone.

He had made his intentions quite obvious. He sought a partner who would help him advance in the parliament and the ton, and she accepted, wanting nothing more than to fulfill his father's expectations. He didn't pretend to know the lady completely, but her peculiar behavior had made him uncomfortable.

Before he proposed, he had to be certain that she would follow him as a devoted wife, refraining from any absurd undertakings till the end of his life. It was customary for persons in his position to find a partner outside of their marriage, and he had no objections as long as the affair was kept secret forever and she delivered him his heir.

He had no reservations about it, but even before they married, the matter would become too sensitive. He should not think about his future bride in this manner, since it may be in his character to constantly prepare for the worst-case situation.

While dancing, Cedric kept his gaze fixed on Lady Vernon in his arms. And, as usual, her eyes seemed to be seeking someone. Initially, he assumed she was overwhelmed or terrified of him since that was the feeling that others expressed in his presence. He never meant to be afraid, but his position had always seemed disrespectful to the other. He was reminded of the days when he didn't have any friends because of his demeanor and had to constantly follow his bigger brother.

When his younger siblings were born, he avoided being with them for fear that they would reject him. He worked really hard to transform himself for a long period. It was all pointless, and his parents had informed him that he didn't have to alter himself to be liked. When his brother embraced him, he stopped trying to be polite to everyone else, instead focusing on his family.

Aside from his family, no one else was unaffected by his overwhelming presence. Cedric drew away when he realized Evelina Winchester showed no signs of being overwhelmed or terrified of him. He chided himself for forgetting that she was the exception.

"Are you alright, my Lord?" He was surprised to hear Lady Vernon speak.

"Pardon me, I am afraid I am not feeling very well," he replied. "Shall we make our way to refreshments?"

"Lead the way, my Lord," she responded, beaming cheerfully. She was already skilled at disguising her emotions, and she would eventually master it just like him. He learned how to seem kind and cheerful among people although all he felt was apathy.

An indifferent man only looked fine in fairy tales, and some ladies admired him for his aloof nature, but while running for a seat in parliament, you must exhibit some emotion since not all conflicts are won via strategy and strength.

He was pleased with himself for how much he had accomplished, and he would go so far as to claim that he had reign of his emotions, and nothing could bother him until he ran into the lady, who irritated him to the point that he wanted to turn away and go.

8

Chapter Eight

Evelina didn't have a specific strategy to get Cedric Whitworth to cooperate with her to uncover the perpetrator despite racking her head for days. There was nothing she could give him to make a bargain, so she chose to befriend him instead. Or she might always irritate him to the point where he has no option but to aid her. Perhaps she should make a bargain to leave him alone forever if he helps her out this time. That seemed nice enough.

Evelina came early to the ball, her gaze locked on the door. She couldn't risk losing him in the throng and missing a chance. She needed to keep an eye on him at all times so that she could take advantage of any opportunities that arose. She waited so long that she began to wonder whether he would even attend the event.

Evelina almost leaped in her seat when she saw him enter the ballroom. She began marching toward him; she had waited long enough and was going to pull him and force him to look her way. She came to a halt when she saw a lady on his arm, and everyone else's attention was drawn to the duo as well. It was an uncommon sighting. She'd never seen him come to the ball with a lady. He only danced with his mother, Lady Whitworth, and his sister-in-law, but she was certain the lady in his arms was not one of them.

Evelina went from behind the shadows toward the couple, who were being hailed by their friends. She had to remain unseen and watch for a while in order to discover who this lady was! Evelina watched them dance; they separated ways but remained within each other's grasp. It was quite frustrating. She may not have the opportunity tonight.

Evelina was becoming irritated. At every ball, Cedric Whitworth was always with that lady. She had no idea he enjoyed attending balls so much. She had worked out who the lady was: the daughter of Lord Vernon, the man who had run against her father for Prime Minister.

She had heard several rumors that they were dating one another and intending to marry shortly. But she wouldn't believe anything unless she heard it from Cedric himself. She felt confident Ton was spreading stories about him.

She needed to do something. If this continues on much longer, she will never be able to complete her objective. She was watching them dance once more on the dance floor when they broke loose and moved towards the refreshments. She had to make her presence known. She felt a sense of accomplishment as Cedric blanched at recognizing her in front of him. She gazed right into his eyes, her lips curling slightly to indicate that she saw through him, and walked away without returning. She hoped he would attempt to find her, but knowing that obstinate man, it was doubtful. She made her presence known to Cedric, and that was enough for tonight.

She was standing on the dimly lighted balcony on the second level, gazing at the stars. Without the moon, the stars were brighter tonight. She stood alone in one of the corners, scrutinizing everyone around her. The women stood in small groups, sometimes gazing at the guys standing a few yards distant, laughing and speaking to one another.

Some of the Lords gazed longingly at the woman they desired, while others were filled with air as a result of their attention. She spotted some of the rare ones who had love-filled eyes for each other. She quickly became bored and glanced at the starry sky.

Somebody coughed behind her. She waved her hand, dismissing the individual, so as not to forget the number of stars in the sky. Before she could finish counting, a large man pulled her into the dark corner.

"My Lady," he said. Even though she couldn't see his face, she knew who it was, and his deep voice proved it. Their eyes were gradually accustomed to the darkness surrounding them and could outline each other. They were invisible to everyone unless they peered extremely closely.

"My Lord," she whispered, looking at him. Her heart began to race; she must be becoming sick. She should get it checked by her old maid. She came to say something, but she couldn't absorb her words.

"You," she said unexpectedly, "I need you." Cedric drew away from the light shining on his face, scrunching up in uncertainty. "We will work together. Yes," she continued, scolding herself to get it together, "We need to discover the perpetrator. Together." He closed his eyes and sighed.

"I am afraid I can't help you, my Lady," he murmured quietly, not wishing to draw attention to them.

"Why not?" She pouted, "Is it because of her?"

He raised his brow, and it dawned on him that she was talking about Lady Vernon. Of course, everyone in the ton had now learned of their romance, and everyone was waiting for the news of their engagement.

"Yes," he said, "It is because I am about to marry. I won't have time to participate in your endeavor, nor would it be suitable."

"But why are you marrying her?" She inquired, shocked that he would marry her.

"And why can't I?" He made a counterattack.

"Well, you both don't look good together," she said.

"And why is that?" He inquired with an edge to his tone.

Evelina didn't know the answer to the question, but she couldn't stand there looking foolish.

"Hair," she said, the first thing that sprang to her.

"Hair?" He expressed his annoyance.

"Yes, you both have dark hair and a pale complexion." If you both wear black, you'll look like a vampire couple, which isn't good," she remarked firmly.

He laughed at her made-up response, making him shine brighter than all the stars she counted, and she was taken aback. She should rush about yelling miracles. Cedric Whitworth could chuckle. She joined him in a tiny chuckle. After a while, they both came to a halt and stood in quiet, staring away from each other.

"Three days from now at noon, meet me at the Hyde garden's back entrance dressed in your disguise," he said after a while.

"Really? Does it imply you're going to aid me?" She inquired enthusiastically.

"I will simply point you in the right direction and after that, you ought to leave me alone," he added.

"But..." she argued.

"That is the deal, take it or leave it," he continued, cutting her short.

"Shake on it," she responded after thinking about it.

"What?" Cedric inquired, stunned.

She offered her exquisite hand as a gentleman's deal. She was a woman, for goodness' sake. But Cedric swallowed his words—after all, she was never ladylike. He slipped her gloved hand into his. She astonished him by shaking his hand firmly. Their hands remained in each other's, and they gradually let go until their fingertips brushed, before walking in opposite ways back to their worlds.

Evelina returned to the ball with butterflies in her stomach. She realized she was in huge danger when she couldn't stop smiling and her face was covered in blush.

Cedric strolled with an uneasy sensation in his heart and a burning trail on his hand.

9

Chapter Nine

Evelina was at Hyde Park's rear entrance, covering her face behind a large hat. She arrived early, waiting for him, her foot tapping quickly on the grass below. He soon emerged from his Whitworth carriage, his gleaming tailcoat shining to match his physique. His black hair was slicked back, and as he approached her, her heart thumped loudly.

Cedric stood in front of her, his gaze searching for someone in the distance.

"My Lady," he said without glancing at her.

"My Lord," she responded.

Evelina came closer, hoping to get him to look at her, but he walked on, leaving her behind. She followed him reluctantly, grumbling.

"There," he said, facing her, "The man with the grey hat and the cigarette in his hand."

"Where?" She inquired, attempting to discover the individual he was referring to. When she didn't hear back from him, she faced him and found him looking at her with wide eyes.

"What is wrong, my Lord?" she said, scrunching her nose.

"Nothing," he responded, shaking his head. "Tell that man you want to buy a horse."

"Why? I don't want to buy a horse," she said honestly.

"He doesn't sell horses, my Lady, it is a secret code," he added. "He is a private investigator; he will find whatever you want to find out for the right price."

"Why the secret code?" She asked, shifting her face to the side.

"His type of work does not comply with the law," Cedric stated.

"Isn't every private investigator the same? I mean, spying on other people's life without their agreement is a felony." She expressed her puzzlement.

"True, my lady," he said. "And hence you ought to give up this foolish quest."

Evelina rolled her eyes, a behavior her mistress was trying hard to break. He wasn't giving up trying to stop her, and she wasn't the kind to give up quickly.

"Thank you for your assistance, even though you were hesitant from the start, my Lord," she added with the greatest respect, tipping her hat in the most gentlemanly way.

"It wasn't a pleasure working with you either, my Lady," Cedric replied with a forced grin. "This is the end of the road for us. I never want to meet you again. Goodbye."

With that, Cedric walked away, while Evelina cursed at him again and headed towards the man standing under the tree.

***

She may report that her encounter with the man went well. Of course, he was horrified about conducting business with a woman, but when she paid him nicely, he performed the song she wanted to hear. He promised to return with a report by the end of the week, and all she had to do now was wait.

"My Lady," Her handmaid called her. "You have a guest."

"A guest?" She expressed amazement, "For me? Are you sure it's not for my mother?"

"No, dear woman. The guest has come to meet with you," her handmaid stated.

"Who in the bloody world wants to meet me?" She murmured while putting on her slippers.

"My Lady," her handmaid interrupted her.

"What is it?" She asked, angry.

"Her Ladyship has asked you to be present in front of the guest, err, in a more appropriate manner," Her handmaid said gently, "I have selected a gown for you and will work on your hairdo. I believe you'll look stunning."

"Ohh, is it!" Evelina gritted her teeth and said, "Is this guest a Lord?"

"Yes, my lady," her handmaid said joyfully.

"Then I must prepare myself, well," Evelina remarked with a phony grin, causing her maid to sigh with relief.

Evelina let the maid beautify her. She had no idea how concealing her freckles on her nose and cheeks with a lot of powder made her seem gorgeous. Instead, she seemed horrible. But if she walks out with her freckles on show, another piece will appear in the ledger about how ugly she was!

"Is everything alright, my Lady?" Her maid inquired, alarmed. "You jerked yourself."

"No, no. I am fine; please continue," Evelina responded. She couldn't inform her maid, so she went to see Cedric Whitworth at midday without disguising her freckles. If her mistress found out she was displaying her freckles in this manner, she would hang her.

She giggled to herself, recalling Cedric Whitworth's stunned reaction when he saw her face. Her maid gave her a troubled expression, which she ignored by waving her hand. Evelina was on her way to one of the balls with her mother and one more nobleman who had just shown an interest in marrying her. She wondered how long he would endure and why he would reject her. Alternatively, he may be a power-hungry leech that she needed to get rid of.

Evelina immediately noticed Lord Cedric Whitworth in the gathering, speaking cordially with his companions. His soon-to-be fiancée was nowhere to be seen. Now, how would she get him to glance at her?

She turned to her friend, who had repeatedly asked her for a dance, which she had flatly declined, much to her mother's dismay.

"My Lord," she murmured, fluttering her eyes, "The dance floor seems to be less crowded than before."

"Yes, it does! Can I have the next dance, my Lady?" He inquired, attempting to project a romantic air. However, Evelina was able to see through his deception.

"That would be my pleasure, please lead the way," she responded. Everyone's attention would be drawn to them since Evelina Winchester had never danced on the ballroom floor. And so, it started!

She was dancing to the music, not with the man holding her, but with the man who could see her from a great distance away. She knew precisely where he was, her glance flitting about him, but as soon as it came close to him, she averted her stare for fear of being caught. He felt cramped in his cravat, his gaze shifting from the talk with his partner to the lady dancing on the floor. The lady who has lately been in his thoughts much more than he would want. He dares not look at the pair on the dance floor, unsure what feelings would arise in his heart.

So, she moved about him, attempting to entangle him, and the unshakable stone-cold statue started to melt.

The dance stopped, and she finally glanced at him. Everything around them blurred. She finally got his attention, but all she could do was depart the scene. Evelina found herself in the library after fleeing the ballroom from that searing look. Her heart was throbbing so loudly that everyone in London could hear it.

When she heard a door click, she turned around to see him in the little room with her. Evelina felt inebriated despite the fact that she was convinced she had not had any sherry today.

She should have greeted him like a respectable lady, but her thoughts were clouded, and all she could do was watch him move forward with slow measured strides.

"Mmm," Evelina said in a squeaky voice. His black eyes glistened with an unfathomable feeling.

He was close to her, the inch that separated them sparking with energy. Her lips opened slightly to breathe in, drawing his attention. He made the first move, lowering his head and taking her lips in his. Then he ravished her lips.

10

Chapter Ten

Cedric was convinced he would go nuts. After kissing Evelina Winchester in the stuffy old library, he packed his belongings and departed London. He was in Silvershire, his duchy, hiding from her and the repercussions of his erratic behavior.

What a poor decision! He should feel embarrassed of himself. He was the image of calm and controlled until he lost control due to an obnoxious lady. Why would he kiss her? He couldn't find a solution, and whenever he thought about it, he couldn't sleep.

It wasn't anything spectacular. He had kissed innumerable women; her lips were not soft, but rather chapped with a strange minty flavor. It was just like any other kiss, a meeting of the lips, yet it sparked a fire in him that never seemed to go out. He went to his mistress to satisfy his wants, but even after that, his mind kept wandering back to her.

After a week of vacation in his Duchy, he couldn't resist the call from London. His party will shortly proclaim the new President and him as Vice President, and his absence at such an occasion would spark unneeded discussion around the community. Cedric was at his office, cleaning up the rubbish. If he had become President, all of his schemes would have fallen through one after another. He gazed at all of the items he had diligently worked on all day and night, hoping they would see the light of day.

"Lord Silvershire." Cedric was surprised by the abrupt entrance. He wasn't taken aback by the lady standing at his door, dressed foolishly to conceal her feminine body. Anyone looking at her could see what she was hiding under those men's clothes. It seemed as if he expected her to show up.

"My Lady," Cedric spoke clearly, "I think I requested you not to exhibit yourself in front of me. Our agreement is complete."

"Our deal was done, and then you broke it," she added, folding her hands.

"How is it that I breached the agreement? I provided you the contact information so you could continue the research," Cedric replied, bored.

"Yes, but then you kissed me in the ball," she added casually, causing his pulse to skip a beat.

He turned around and buried his face in the bookcase behind his chair, seeking nothing in particular.

"About that, it was a mistake," Cedric was lost for words. "It is best we forget about it."

"Absolutely not," she said. He was perplexed by her reaction. He realized that he was the one who kissed her, and he should apologize to her face. When his eyes met hers, he saw purity he had never seen before. His imagination was playing tricks on him; this wild cyclone of a lady couldn't possibly be as innocent as she seemed.

"What do you mean?" He asked instead.

"You kissed me," she continued. "It was my first kiss and I hardly remember what happened let alone enjoy it." Cedric swallowed; he felt like he was on the gallows, about to be punished for stealing her first kiss. "I demand you kiss me again," she said. Cedric believed he was either dreaming or hallucinating. This lady hadn't simply requested he kiss her so casually. He laughed in disbelief.

"My Lady," Cedric murmured, uncertain of his words, "Have you lost your goddamn mind?"

"You took my first kiss without my permission and now have the audacity to ask me if I have lost my mind," She admonished, "I just need to comprehend that all they say in the literature is accurate about the first kiss. Unfortunately, I cannot make sense of it. I need you to kiss me again to be sure."

Cedric got caught up in something unexpected, and for the first time in his life, he couldn't figure out how to cope with it. He needed a drink.

He approached the decanter, as Evelina settled on the chair in front of his desk.

"What is this?" She spoke after a while, clutching a piece of paper.

Cedric returned to his table, assembling his preparations. After all, she was his adversary's daughter.

"Are you here to spy on me?" He asked sincerely.

"Do you think I am stupid to tell you if I was spying on you?" She replied.

"Right! Where is your brain, Cedric?" "Personal Property Bill: The noblewoman's right to own property independent of her husband and children," she read aloud from the paper she had stolen.

"Give that back," he said, reaching out to seize it.

"Are you serious about this?" She expressed amazement.

"I wondered whether I would have been President. Not anymore," he stated, removing the paper and tucking it into a file.

"You mean the ladies of the ton could have their own estate?" she said, still following him about like a lost puppy.

"Yes," he responded, placing the last parchments in the file.

"The estates owned by the ladies of the house," she went on to say.

"Yes, my Lady," he groaned.

"That is ridiculous," she said casually.

"And why is that?" He inquired, insulted.

"Woman can't manage the estate, it is the job of the estate's Lord," she added with a smile.

"Isn't the woman aware of all the affairs of the estate?" He asked.

"Yes, but men make all the decisions," she said.

"That doesn't mean women are incapable of making those decisions themselves," he remarked. "It is simply that they aren't given the freedom to make those decisions."

"If women were capable of making choices, they should have been present in decision-making environments. We don't even have female butlers," she proudly said.

"Maybe we should start with that," he suggested.

"What if the women don't want it? What if they do not want to make such decisions?" She asked.

"And why wouldn't they?" He countered, "You are the sole child of Lord Winchester. Don't you become furious or disappointed that your father's duchy will go to some unknown stranger? Won't you want to keep the home where you were born and raised and manage it as you see fit rather than handing it away to a stranger when you marry?"

"Well, my father's duchy will belong to my cousin, who I know quite well. He is a good man; he is perfectly capable of looking after the duchy," she remarked. "And even if he wasn't, I don't want to be in a situation where I had to make major judgments. It is a Lord's job; a lady cannot do it."

"You're your father's daughter. You're conservative people. I never expected you to understand," he remarked dismissively.

"Neither do you," she said. "The only women who own the estate are the shameful mistresses of Lords. No respectable noble lady wishes to be in this position."

"And have you asked all the respectable noble ladies of the ton?" he inquired sarcastically.

"Have you?" She sassed back.

"I know of one and one is enough for me," he replied.

"And who that might be?" She remarked, expecting him to mention his lover, which would entirely undermine his thesis.

"My mother," he said gently.

11

Chapter Eleven

"Your mother," Evelina said, surprised, "Lady Whitworth."

"Yes," he said, his eyes expressing grief for a second.

"You must be jesting," she said with a giggle. "She is the Duchess of Whitworth, why would she want to be mistress of another estate?"

"Not the mistress, only the master," he clarified.

"Then does she want to be the sole master of the Duchy of Whitworth?" She inquired with a raised eyebrow.

"No, not Whitworth. Silvershire," he said.

"Silvershire. Aren't you the Duke of Silvershire?" She asked, confused.

"I am," he said.

"I do not understand," she replied.

"I suppose so,"

"Then explain," she said in an apparent tone.

"Why?" He questioned, disinterested.

"Because I want to understand," she said, astonished.

He looked at her attentively, seeing nothing except a sincere desire to learn.

"It is quite a story," he moaned, and she sat calmly, her ears pricked up and her face was intrigued. He took a big breath. Nobody ever enquired about his or his brother's titles. Why were they all Dukes even if they weren't firstborn?

She was the first, and he couldn't help but recount the story.

"My maternal grandfather was the youngest prince and he loved his daughter dearly," he said.

Prince Windsor considered his daughter to be the greatest treasure. He reared her with gentleness and an open mind. As she grew older and reached marriageable age, he was certain that no man, least of all the free-spirited Lord Whitworth, could ever be suitable for her. Despite his disapproval of her spouse, he couldn't stand in the way of his daughter's happiness.

He wanted her to be her own person, the mistress of her own life. He gave her the Duchy of Silvershire, a royal duchy under his care. However, the law does not allow a woman to be the estate owner, and the prince would never connect his daughter's gift to Whitworth. After recognizing that convincing his daughter not to marry Whitworth would be futile,

Prince Windsor sought help from everyone. Finally, it was determined that the second son of Whitworth, who would never inherit the Whitworth Duchy, would become master of the Silvershire.

Even though Cedric became Duke of Silvershire as soon as he was born, Silvershire will always remain his mother's, independent from Whitworth. Her unique existence in the world is unrelated to anybody. Any other woman would have been terrified, but she was a natural queen who was overjoyed at the prospect of being a master, but in the eyes of society, her identity was tied to her husband and boys.

"Why is it necessary for a woman's identity to be connected to a man? Why is she always a daughter, a wife, or a mother, rather than just herself?" he inquired. "My mother is considerably more skilled and brilliant than half of the men in parliament, and she will be recognized only as the Duchess of Whitworth. She will never be able to convey her thoughts to anybody or actively participate in King's Council or Parliament meetings. Her brilliance will always remain buried, and she will eventually forget what she is capable of. Don't get me wrong, my Lady; my mother is perfectly content with Whitworth Duchy, and my father loves her more than everything in the world, but a part of her will always remain unsatisfied."

He exhaled. He realized he had spoken too much, but he couldn't help but say a little more.

"My mother was fortunate to have my father, but it made me think about all the other women who are less fortunate. Who grudgingly have to give up all for their spouse. Worthless husbands squander their wives' riches on mistresses and gambling, leaving the ladies in misery."

Evelina was perplexed. She could not accept anything he said. Lady Whitworth was the embodiment of elegance and grandeur for all ladies in Great Britain, and no one was aware of the other side of the coin. If the truth is revealed, it will be a much worse scandal than anything witnessed previously. Everything he said contradicted what she had been taught. A respectable woman marries a noble Lord, produces an offspring to carry on his lineage, and devotes herself to caring for her husband's family. Ton glanced at her mother as if she had produced a difficult daughter rather than an heir. How many times have her family begged her father to choose another woman who can deliver an heir? A mistress son will be enough, they would remark.

"Did your mother tell you this?" She inquired after a protracted quiet.

"She does not have to. She adored the Duchy of Silvershire, which was clear when she began grooming me for the post. She constantly inspired me to be more than just a Duke. It may surprise you, but my passion for politics stems from her."

He spoke affectionately, a shadow of a grin on his lips, completely engrossed in his surroundings. It was difficult for her to comprehend what he said, yet his enthusiasm made him seem otherworldly. She saw something in him that compelled people to follow him when he talked.

"My father is admired and honored by royalty for his brilliant methods, but no one realizes that my mother was at the center of it all. She settled on the most efficient one, closing all the loopholes and being able to think far into the future," he said. "My mother was usually by my father's side, labouring in the shadows. She was his brain, and he is her strength. They make a formidable team."

He paid close attention to the emotions that flowed over her face. It was amusing to see the spectrum of emotions flowing through while attempting to grasp. She was having trouble digesting anything she heard.

"It is time you leave, my Lady," he murmured after she remained quiet for a long period.

"But I have more questions," she said.

"Even if I answer all of your questions you won't understand," he said.

"And why not?" She grumbled.

"Because of your," He paused in mid-sentence. Evelina felt her heart break a little. "My parents," she added with a false confidence, "You may say anything. I know you were thinking about it."

"It is not like that," He murmured quietly. "I apologize."

He'd seen through her façade.

"I know my parents are traditionalists, the most conservative members of the family. But I never felt like I lacked anything in their care," she said.

"And yet here you are on a whimsical adventure that I am sure your parents will be horrified to learn about," he shouted, returning to his normal sarcasm.

"I never said they were perfect," Evelina began, feeling anxious about discussing her parents in front of others. Especially because he was not just her father's opponent, but also hailed from a family whose parents seemed to be without problems.

Cedric overheard her. He sat down in his chair and gave her the glass of water. She was in anguish, and he asked her to hold and console her.

"My parents seem so incompetent to you but they love me and they have never done anything that I do not like," she went on to say. "What's wrong with being conservative? I'm from this land, and I want to uphold age-old customs. I am a proud Englishman."

"And yet your name is not English at all," he smugly said.

Chapter Twelve

The season was in full swing. Every aristocrat attended the balls and soirees as if their lives depended on it. Christmas was coming, and it was a season of joy and celebration. But for Cedric, it was time to labour till the bone crunched before parliament took a break until the New Year. He was in his study at the Whitworth mansion.

He twisted the piece of paper in his hand in preparation for the inheritance bill. He had planned every aspect of getting the measure presented to parliament once he became the party's President, but now all he could do was drink his whiskey on a lonely night.

He returned the paper to his files and proceeded to the parlour, where his parents, Hannah, and Percival were relaxing by the fireplace.

His younger brothers had yet to visit the house, gallivanting from one ball to another and enjoying the life they desired.

"Cedric, darling," his mother said. "Come and sit with us. Let me ask the chef to bring you one of the exquisite cream ices he made today."

"Thank you, Mother," he said, getting himself comfortable.

"Mother, you should taste the cream ice from the south gate of Hyde Park, it is more delicious than anything you have ever tasted," Percival said.

"Oh, we understand. Your father and I used to frequent that tiny cream ice store," his mother added, "Maybe you might take Hannah for a stroll in the park and have some excellent cream ice."

Percival and Hannah exchanged knowing smiles as a secret passed between them, leaving Cedric with a sensation of desire. He had always prioritized his profession above love and family, but at times like this, he wondered if he could have it all. Evelina gradually penetrated his head, and he made no attempt to ignore her presence. He was aware of his attraction to her, and as long as he did not act on it, he was secure.

He just noticed that he was observing Evelina at every party and soiree he went to, and his gaze was invariably drawn to her among the throng. And every time they met, he made a point of addressing her as Lady Evelina and watching as the color of her hair gradually matched the color of her neck. It irritated him so much that she had ceased visiting his office in parliament or ambushing him while disguised. Every time they met, her face was caked with that terrible powder, concealing her beauty underneath it. He wanted to see those freckles on her nose and cheeks again and etch them into his mind.

He was looking forward to seeing her at the royal Christmas event, which his family was attending. As youngsters, they would always accompany their parents to the palace, and he was familiar with practically all of the hidden chambers and corridors owing to his younger brother's mischief. He intended to utilize them, to relax and enjoy the holidays, rather than stressing about or preparing for the second parliament season.

He intended to spend his whole Christmas break harassing Evelina. He wanted to stay looking at her as she counted the stars, count the freckles on her adorable tiny nose and cheeks, and kiss and ravish her to his heart's delight.

He knew what he desired was not achievable, but merely spending time with her away from prying eyes and hiding from everyone seemed like nirvana. The idea of a covert meeting intrigued him.

Cedric was well-dressed and impatiently waited for his family to arrive at the palace. He was riding behind Percival and Hannah in their carriage. The air around them felt unpleasant, and he wanted to get out of there as quickly as possible. He sprang out of the carriage as it struck the palace ground. He waited for Percival and Hannah to go ahead, then followed them at the necessary distance to preserve the hierarchy. The ballroom was exquisitely adorned, as anticipated of the royals. Hannah would halt in the midst to admire the beauty, whilst Percival would gaze at her as if no beauty could ever compare to her.

His eyes were unconcerned with the ballroom's design or his brother's undying love for his wife, which he had begun to covet. His eyes were already searching for her. It wouldn't be simple to detect her. Every moment she got away from her mother and mistress, she disappeared on her own whimsical trip, and he longed to be with her and partake in her experiences. Cedric intended to go seek for her, but he was quickly stopped by a few of his coworkers.

He was preoccupied. For the first time, he refused to speak out on politics and parliament. He was becoming agitated, his fingers firmly clutched in his hand, and his countenance reflected the fury he was feeling as a result of the delay.

"My Lord," he heard her say, her voice giving him shivers all over. He could sense her presence right behind him, yet he remained still, like a stone statue.

"Lady Winchester," someone said, "What brings you here?" Cedric's gaze remained unwaveringly fixed forward.

"Have you seen my father?" She added softly, "I seem to have lost him in the throng. I recall you being at my father's side earlier."

"Oh, I think he might be around somewhere, how about a dance till your father makes an appearance, my Lady?" the individual said.

"I saw him walking towards the queen's rose garden," Cedric said stoically, without glancing back at her.

She thanked everyone and went away. She'd found him. She always seemed to find him; a faint grin appeared on his lips.

He immediately excused himself and proceeded to where he knew she would be. He hurriedly proceeded down the corridors towards the rose garden, but his attention was drawn by a thud from one of the doors.

He would have gone away immediately if he hadn't heard a woman's voice. He moved gently towards the door, cautiously twisting the knob and slipping inside. He walked toward the chamber's private corner, making sure the door remained open.

He was startled to see his fiancée, Lady Vernon, in the arms of another man. Her eyes closed in pleasure, and she threw her head back. Cedric felt he had to go before the pair regained their wits. Then he felt a little warm hand slide into his palm and softly grasp it.

As he watched the woman he was supposed to marry kissing another man, he tried to summon any emotions to feel, but all he felt was indifference, until this annoying woman who came following him held his hand to comfort him, and everything in front of him blurred as he became lost in the sensation of her hands on his and the sensation that ran through his palms to the entire body. She gently drew him away, softly locking the door and fleeing someplace, and he understood this was the lady he would joyfully and voluntarily follow for the rest of his life.

13

Chapter Thirteen

They were hiding away in the queen's garden. Thick shrubs encircled them, keeping them hidden from the outside world, while the moon shined brilliantly in the sky, lighting everything around them. They stood, gathering their breath. No one would know they were there unless they were seeking this specific location.

They gazed at one another, panting, her eyes troubled, while he observed her beneath the stars. No one spoke for a long time since it seemed wrong to interrupt their moment with an unneeded sound. It was lovely; the music from the ball would float towards them, like a thread connecting them to the actual world. Cedric was immediately aware of the energy surging around them.

"Lady Everly," he said hurriedly. As predicted, she snarled at him, shattering the trance established over them.

"It's Evelina, not Everly," she replied, annoyed.

"But you are English, are you not?" He inquired, teasingly.

"Yes," she said.

"Evelina is not an English name," he said smugly.

"I know," she responded, bored up with his mocking, "I'm named after the Spanish Princess."

"Is that what your parents told you, Lady Everly?" He taunted her again.

"They told me the story too," she remarked, folding her arms in annoyance at him.

"Pray, tell me too," he begged, mirroring her childish behavior.

She stared at him curiously. Cedric Whitworth was chatting frivolously with her. It nearly made her feel unique, but she knew he wouldn't spend his time learning the tale behind her name. It's likely he sought to divert himself from the situation he saw his fiancée in.

"The Crown Prince of Britain was engaged to the Crown Princess of Spain, Princess Evelina," she claimed.

"Pardon my interruption, my Lady," he replied. She sighed, unhappy with the intrusion.

"What is the problem, my Lord?" She asked, irritated.

"Princess Beatrice, not Princess Evelina, is the Spanish Princess who was betrothed to and later married our Crown Prince. I've never heard of any Princess Evelina," he stated sincerely.

"If you hadn't interrupted me, you would have known who Princess Evelina was," she replied with a smirk.

"Please proceed, my Lady," he responded, surprised. "I will not interrupt you any further."

"So, when Princess Evelina was born, she was already betrothed to the British Crown Prince. The two kingdoms formed an alliance via their betrothal. The alliance that brought wealth to Britain." She planned to marry the Crown Prince in Britain when she was sixteen, but the civil war in Spain jeopardized the marriage, so she fled her family at the age of ten. My father was the one who met her on the coast of Agagusus. He was a vital figure in forming the alliance and was the first to see the Princess on English soil; he was overjoyed, so much so that he abandoned his wife in labour to welcome her."

"But the adversaries were merciless; they sunk the Princess' boat in the middle of the ocean, and her body could not be retrieved. My father returned despondent with the news that shocked both Britain and Spain. The partnership was in peril. With their Princess gone and civil conflict raging, Spain was unable to transmit the money promised to Britain, perhaps sparking a civil war in Britain."

"I was born the day Princess died and my father so fond of the Princess he never met but thought of as a saviour named me after her and soon became the Prime Minister of Britain forging a new alliance."

"Then the current Princess?" Cedric inquired quietly. He was unaware of the story of Princess Evelina. He just knew Princess Beatrice married the Crown Prince to form an alliance.

"She hadn't even been born when Princess Evelina died. However, it was resolved that any Princess born in Spain would become Queen of England, receiving the financial benefits that Spain had long promised Britain. Princess Beatrice was engaged to the Crown Prince even before she opened her eyes to the world; it's no surprise she was hesitant to marry."

Cedric listened to her intently. She, like her father, seemed to be fond of Princess Evelina.

"And now you know, my name is Evelina, not anything else," Evelina asserted.

"Yes, my lady," Cedric grinned, and she smiled back. They grinned at each other for quite a while. The lighting flickered as cool air hit them, making her tremble. They sat there in quiet in one other's company, and that was enough.

"We should return to the ball; our absence will be noticed shortly," he replied hesitantly.

"Can't we just stay here looking at the flickering candles and the stars above and watch the sunrise?" She asked longingly.

"I am afraid, we can't, ever." He stated with a downcast expression. She said nothing.

"Please make your way to the ball, my Lady. I'll wait a few minutes to avoid raising any suspicion," he added.

"Alright," she responded, standing up, "I will see you around, my Lord." She gave a beautiful curtsy before turning around and leaving through the hiding bushes.

"You too, Lady Evelina," He muttered, his words reaching her clearly in the calm night, but she dared not return to him since she was certain she would be unable to leave again. Cedric didn't return to the ball. He joined his younger brother in gambling and drinking. He knew if he saw her again, his heart would split in two. He would be unable to dance or kiss her gloved hands.

This was the end of their relationship; he was convinced he loved her. She was the kind of woman he would never marry, yet now he wanted to spend every moment with her. The issue was not that he was in love with her; he might have loved her and remained distant; the issue was that she returned his love. Evelina may not have understood her sentiments, but he could tell by the way she looked at him and smiled that she was also drawn to him. And this made him unable to remain away. If she continues to pursue him, it will be very difficult for him to let her go.

He needed a diversion, anything to take her out of his head, at least briefly. His fiancé's affair with another member of his party should be enough of a distraction. He had to make certain that no one else found out about her romance, and that it ended before it might jeopardize his plans for her to marry him and, ultimately, what her father promised him.

When the night was over, Cedric couldn't recall how much he drank to keep Evelina out of his head. He awoke on his younger brother's land, head-heavy and mouth dry. He rang the bell, intending to sleep again after he had eaten some meal.

As always, he was offered tea, cookies, and the Ledger on the side. He requested breakfast and drank his tea, trying to relieve his headache. He took up the ledger to see what London was up to till late at night.

"Lord Winchester's only daughter finally set to marry"

Lord Winchester announced the engagement of his daughter, Lady Evelina, to Lord Reginald of the Conservative Party. The news was delivered to a select group of friends during the Royal Christmas Ball.

14

Chapter Fourteen

Cedric was in a slump. The announcement of the new Liberal Party President occurred just before the second Parliament session began. He stopped leaving his estate; he should have been preparing for parliament, but instead submitted himself to spirits.

His family was concerned about him. Every day, he received a visit from one or more family members. They did not attempt to engage him in conversation or compel him to improve. They realized that he needed time to grieve the loss of his goal. He slept all day and awoke to his mother splashing a pail of water on his face. After berating him for the whole dusk and forcing him to shave and clean up his act, as well as eat his lunch, Cedric felt alive.

His mother sat him down like he was a youngster and explained to him that there is more than one method to attain one's goals. Being a party leader was only one path to his goal; he now has to find another. She was positive that, of all her children, he was the one who would always overcome whatever obstacles that came his way. He was thankful to his mother, but the Presidency was never far from his thoughts.

His mother departed shortly after, and he requested that more brandy be brought into his room. He was sipping on his glass of spirits when his butler rushed in, reporting that someone had come to see him. He sprung up, believing it was his mother again, and quickly started placing decanters behind the seats.

"What are you doing?" He paused as he heard a voice outside his door. Ah, his mother was correct. He'd fully lost it. He had reached his limit in hearing her in his room, and when he saw her standing inside his bed-chamber, he knew he had begun hallucinating.

"My Lord," His butler spoke out, standing just behind her with a troubled expression.

Before he could answer, she told him to bring whiskey to his room and settled upon the sofa in front of him as if it were her own bed-chamber. The feelings he'd been repressing with the booze had begun to pound on his heart's door, demanding to be let out.

She sat in front of him in her disguise, which could hardly conceal her thin frame, her red hair tangled owing to the hat's inability to control it, and her face gleaming with the gorgeous freckles on show.

His pulse was pounding so loudly that he could hear it resonating throughout his chamber. His butler poured the whiskey for her and stepped to the side.

"You may go now. I am not going to jeopardize your Lordship," she said smugly. Following Cedric's signal, his butler left them alone. They drank their beverages in the solitude of the darkroom, where a fire crackled on the hearth.

"I didn't expect to find you in such a state, my Lord," she murmured, facing him again. He straightened himself, hoping she didn't see him gazing at her. "This is definitely worse than I expected," she continued when he didn't answer.

"What are you doing here, my Lady?" He inquired, his voice husky.

"What are you doing here?" She questioned him back. "Shouldn't you be introducing your bill for the inheritance for ladies in the parliament or announcing that your engagement to Lady Vernon is off?" Cedric downed the last of the brandy.

"And why would I do any of it?" He asked gently. She gave him a doubting look, which made him uneasy. He poured himself another tumbler of brandy. He shouldn't have been drinking so much; he was losing control, but he wanted to flee away even more. He was extending it too far, and when anything is pushed to its maximum, it breaks.

Evelina was concerned and upset by the condition in which she discovered him. She never expected him to drink away his grief. After checking for him at every ball and waiting for him to arrive at parliament when the second session began, he was still missing. He vanished without a trace. She waited eagerly for the news that he had broken off his engagement after finding another fiancée. But it appeared he was never going to call off his engagement. How could he imagine spending his whole life with someone who was with someone else while engaged to him? Wasn't she the same? Her father had proclaimed her engagement, but now she was in the chamber of another man.

Maybe we were all the same; we can't have the one we want, and she craved Cedric from the bottom of her heart.

She went mad because he was nowhere to be found. She wanted to see him and feel his presence. She sought even the tiniest contact, and she longed to experience their first kiss again. After Cedric kissed Evelina for the first time, she was exposed to the realm of magic, and she fell in love with kissing him and wanted to kiss him forever.

"When will you kiss me again?" Evelina's unexpected statements startled Cedric. Her words hit him like a pail of water, as he was fully awake. He glanced at her with wide eyes. He swallowed at the serious expression on her face; she was not joking with him. She demanded a kiss from him. He blinked quickly, attempting to come up with an answer.

He didn't say anything, sitting tightly in his seat, scared he'd lose all control at any moment. He took long breaths to calm himself. He needed to handle this cautiously since she had been drinking spirits and he had lost track of how much she had in her system.

"Don't you want to kiss me?" She inquired, her expression softening. She appeared like an angel imploring him to transgress.

"You do not understand what you are asking for," he complained.

"I understand. I am asking for a kiss," she said boldly.

"Do you understand the implications of asking for a kiss from a man like this?" He stated with scant composure.

"Are you going to refer to me as a wanton woman? Because, as far as I know, a wanton woman is the one who continues to kiss every other man, but I just want to kiss you," she said honestly.

His heart skipped a beat when she made her nonchalant revelation. She was unaware of the emotions that ran uncontrolled within him. He wanted to ask her what she meant when she said she simply wanted to kiss him, but knowing how whimsical she was, he assumed she said it without thinking, and he'd prefer not to open the door, which would cause discomfort for both of them or crush his heart even more.

"So? What's your decision?" She inquired again, sipping on her whiskey.

"Go home, my Lady," He replied dismissively, without looking at her. He approached his window, hand clenched, and evened out his breathing. The moon was quite brilliant.

"What about my kiss?" She inquired again from behind him. He wanted the ground to swallow him; the gentleman in him couldn't give her what she desired, but the beast in him wanted to utterly possess her.

"It is so surprising, you want to fight the world for the things no woman has asked of you and yet you deny my wish," she remarked with a smirk.

In the Arms of a Rake Series

"Your wish is a kiss, correct?" He asked, still gazing at the moon.

"Yes," she answered enthusiastically.

"I can't stop at a kiss."

15

Chapter Fifteen

Evelina was in the seventh heaven. The night was wonderful. There was just she, him, and the moon. Every spot he touched still tingled, and each kiss lit a fire inside her. Even the simplest remembrance of the night made her shudder and grin. She felt as if she were floating.
"Lady Evelina," her lady's maid said as she entered her house.
"Yes," Evelina said, not attempting to disguise her grin. "What is it?" She asked excitedly.
"They are waiting for you in the study, my Lady," Her maid said gravely.
Evelina's joy faded into a scowl as she realized who was waiting for her. She paled, panic seizing her heart, knowing that nothing good awaited her. She knocked twice on the study door and then entered.

As predicted, her father sat in his normal spot, while her mother stood near the shelves, holding a glass of red wine. She was aware that her mother had once again expressed concern about her drinking so early in the morning.

But she didn't appreciate her fiancé, Lord Vaughn, standing in her study as if he owned it. Her anxiety changed to frustration, and she clenched her teeth.

"Evy," her father said, making her stand straight.

"Yes, father," she said gently. Her father's appearance urged her to act like a lady. She had never been terrified of anything, but the circumstance she was in made her stomach sink.

"Lady Evelina, my beloved fiancée," Lord Adam remarked, "You spent the whole night; please tell me you discovered anything valuable." Evelina would have put herself in the position of being terrified of her parents, but she would not allow him to intimidate her.

"My Lord, please forgive my tardiness," she added with a mocking smirk, "But Lord Silvershire can certainly keep up with liquor, unlike someone we know."

"I must ask if you are better than Lord Silvershire in keeping up with liquor or if your father lied when he said you remain unaffected by alcohol," he replied with a wry grin. Evelina balled her fists. How dare he!

"It is very handy. There is no place to say you made a mistake because you were inebriated," he said.

Evy narrowed her eyes and would have struck him in the face if her father hadn't interrupted her.

"Evy," her father said, "Did you find anything important in his estate?"

"How would she know what is important and what is not, my Lord," Lord Adam remarked, insulting her.

"Evy, please let us know all that you found we will decide if you really succeeded in finding something of use," he stated dismissively.

"It is Lady Evelina to you," she replied, her eyes mirroring the flames.

"We are not married yet, and Lady Evelina will be yours until that day."

"What difference does it make if it is before or after the wedding day? We're getting married," he responded, furious with her for speaking to him disrespectfully.

"We'll see," Evy said under her breath.

A period of stillness occurred in the study.

"My Lord, what about your mission?" She inquired vindictively. He gazed at her with scorn and tightened his hand at his side.

"We didn't find anything important in his office," he said, gritting his teeth.

"So, my daughter doesn't need to spy on him anymore. She needs to start with wedding preparations," Evelina's mother said.

"But," Evelina and Lord Adam said simultaneously, gazing at one other.

"If there was nothing at his parliamentary office, it must have been in his estate. I can't believe Lord Silvershire had nothing to break in parliament;

now that he isn't even President, he has nothing to lose." Lord Adam responded, "He has already lost to his own party."

Lord Adam enraged Evelina by speaking so negatively about Cedric. Her rage, however, was unjustified; Cedric seemed dejected, and she did not want to leave him alone at this moment. She must find a way to remain with him.

"There is definitely something," she remarked, pondering.

"Well, I doubt you brought something useful," Lord Adam remarked.

"What is it, Evy?" Her father inquired, disregarding Lord Adam.

"Well, I am not sure what it is. However, once elected President, he planned to bring something significant to parliament. I believe he will need some time to recover from the loss of the Presidency before presenting his face in parliament," she remarked with a straight face.

"And what is this big thing?" Lord Adam inquired carefully.

"I don't know, my Lord," Evelina said. "He's keeping quiet about it."

"Then you should find out. This is critical for us," he replied angrily.

"But the wedding preparations, my Lord," she remarked, faking concern.

"Our moms can handle that. You must infiltrate Whitworth Manor; he must have kept those documents in his home," Lord Adam said.

"Very well, my Lord," she said, "If father agrees with this then I will continue to spy on Cedric Whitworth."

She gazed at her father with anticipation. Her father narrowed his eyes at her since she recognized what she was up to. "Lord Winchester, I'd want to let my betrothed continue spying on Cedric Whitworth. In the long run, this will benefit us all," Lord Adam said. His tone suggested he had more influence over her as his future bride than her father had over her as his daughter. It infuriated Evelina, but it was the only way she could be near to Cedric for the time being.

"Very well, but the wedding preparation must go on," the Earl said. "I would like for the wedding to happen immediately after the Prince's ball."

"I agree, my Lord," Lord Adam answered. "I'll depart immediately. I believe you have complete control."

"Evy," Lord Adam approached her and took her gloved hand in his.

"Lady Evelina," she repeated.

"I will see you soon, my darling," he whispered, kissing the back of her hand.

He walked away while Evelina cursed his disappearing form. She had to go before her parents could interrogate her.

"What are you hiding?" She heard her father as she moved to walk away. She turned around and faced her parents.

"What do you mean, father?" She asked, attempting to seem innocent.

"Do not try to be smart with me, young lady," Lord Winchester remarked. "What are you hiding?"

Evelina realized it was pointless to lie to her father. She could not conceive of a plausible lie.

"Lord Cedric Whitworth is set to marry Lady Vernon," she said, determined to tell the truth.

When she didn't say anything, her father waited for her to speak again.

"Everyone is aware of that, Evy," Lady Winchester responded. "There is something more, isn't it?"

"Lady Vernon is having an affair with the new President of the Liberal Party. Lord Silvershire is aware of it, and I'm not sure why, yet he is determined to marry her."

Her look changed to one of annoyance. Her parents stared at one other, concerned about their daughter. Evelina saw the gaze they gave each other. Perhaps she should get away from this horrible mess. She did not want Cedric to be with a lying whore, and she was confident that her father would use this knowledge to harm Cedric, making it impossible for him to marry Lady Vernon. Her parents' anxious expressions made her feel guilty. Her parents' disappointment weighed heavily on her heart. She may choose whether to make them or herself happy.

Perhaps it was time to let him go?

16

Chapter Sixteen

They avoided each other for some time. They both were in the arms of others, aching to be with one another. They planned their future with others and fantasized about living it together. When they saw someone else staring at them, their eyes welled up with tears. They danced with others while envisioning themselves together. They were constantly aware of each other's presence but could only remain in their position, feet firmly planted on the earth. Their hearts would race to each other, but there was a line they couldn't cross. It was the most horrific kind of torture.

They were getting ready for the wedding, but their vows would be for someone else. They were becoming more unhappy with each passing day.

As the day progressed, the gap between them widened, but the love in their hearts increased exponentially. Cedric submerged himself in Parliamentary work to ignore the sorrow in his heart, while Evelina gradually lost her spirit. She spent much of her time in her rooms, napping or assisting her mother with wedding preparations. They couldn't believe it had been so long since she bravely and naively went to his mansion and demanded that he pay for his wrongdoing. Her wedding date was postponed since her fiancé and father were winding up parliament's second session.

One gloomy winter night, she was lounging in her bedchamber, fumbling through her books, when her maid reported Lord Vaughn' arrival. He was waiting in the study. She didn't bother dressing up, annoyed at him for bothering her so late at night. She barged into the study, where he had put himself at ease. Evelina's rage became even stronger when she witnessed him using her house as if it were his own, ordering about her servants and visiting when her parents were abroad.

"What brings you here, my Lord?" She questioned arrogantly; her blanket snugly wrapped around her.

"Your incompetency," he replied. Evelina glanced at him with disbelief.

"Do you think you will be let off the hook whenever you wish for it, Evy?" He remarked, setting his glass of whiskey on the table. He approached her, his gaze predatory. Evelina knew danger was approaching, but all she could do was freeze in place.

In the Arms of a Rake Series

"After I instructed you to continue spying on Cedric Whitworth, you stopped meeting him completely. Do you get ideas on your own? Your brain is not to think; it is only to accept and execute my commands," he said. "Don't think I haven't been keeping an eye on you."

"You have been spying on me," she responded, shocked. He chuckled menacingly, instilling terror in her heart.

"You naive foolish girl," Lord Adam exclaimed disgustedly. "You think it was an accident your father found out about you and that bastard Whitworth."

He was standing in front of her, and his terrible breath made her nauseated.

"No, my future bride," he added, "I was the one who planned everything. I knew spying on you would assist me, but I never expected to become Lord of Winchester and Prime Minister of this nation."

"You bastard," Evelina scoffed. He gripped her face tightly, his fingers pushing into her cheeks. She strained against him, using all her might to pull him off of her.

"You whore," He yelled. "You think anybody would want to marry such a nasty and unattractive lady as you? You can't keep a man at your side even with that wealthy dowry, and you don't have anything that a man would find appealing. You better be glad that I offered to marry you. This Duchy is insufficient for anybody to marry the likes of you."

Evelina's dread and wrath swirled together, and all she could think of was getting out of his grip. Evelina's thoughts were racing wild. She searched her mind for anything to aid her. She wasn't sure whether it would actually help, but it was her final option.

She took a deep breath and kicked his crotch with her knees, causing him to collapse to the ground in great agony. She finally breathed correctly, and he attempted to take her by the hem of her garment.

She fled before he could approach her. She dashed along the corridors toward the stable. She knocked on the stable boy's door and urged him to ready her carriage immediately. Her home was unsafe for her, and she wanted to leave. She wanted to go somewhere he couldn't catch her.

"My Lady," the stable boy murmured worriedly, not daring to question his mistress, "Where to?"

"Lord Silvershire estate," she said, holding her nightgown firmly about her.

The night was chilly and nasty. Every bend on the cobblestone street, every whisper in her ears, and every bump on the road sparked panic in her spike. She glanced around quickly before dashing to his mansion door. She hammered on his door, waking up half of the staff. His butler answered the door violently but quickly welcomed her inside once he recognized her. She was trembling from head to toe, with her hair sticking out everywhere, and dressed inappropriately. She rushed to Cedric's room the moment she walked inside. His butler dashed after her, imploring her to halt, which just accelerated her pace.

She barged into his room like she often did, but this time she was terrified and wanted to fall into his arms and weep her heart out. She envisioned him reclining on the sofa, drinking whiskey and perusing papers in front of the fireplace.

But the sight in front of her was worse than anything she had experienced so far. He was resting with nude inside the sheets on his bed, while a half-naked lady stood at the window, holding a glass of wine. Evelina felt her world collapsing.

All of the murmurs, insults, and accusations that she was stupid ran through her mind. She went back the steps she had taken, the vision in front of her blurred with tears in her eyes, Cedric's voice coming from far away, and she wanted to go far away so she would never hear it again. She rushed down the halls as quickly as her legs could carry her, but he was quicker. He held her in his grip tightly enough not to let her go, but loose enough for her to fight and kick him. He held her as she sobbed and wrecked in his arms. He held her till she calmed down, her sobs reduced to hiccups.

He held her till she had exhausted herself. He held her in his arms till she fell asleep in the hallway.

He brought her into his bedroom and put her on his bed. Her body was still trembling while she slept. He wanted to hug her to stop her shaking, but he knew she would be disgusted by him when she awoke.

Her pleas revealed that she was suffering a nightmare, which shattered his heart. She was helpless.

He sat alongside his bed, clutching her hand as she slept, hoping to take away her nightmares and make them his.

17

Chapter Seventeen

It was early morning. The sun's rays were making their way to the ground, lighting everything with a golden glow and bringing gloom back into the shadows. Evelina awoke feeling bewildered and nauseous. She sat up, her head hammering, her throat dry, and she had a terribly unpleasant sensation within. A glass of water was brought to her lips, and she drank it thirstily, her fingers gripping the glass hard and her hands wrapping around his.

The silence between them was like a solid wall. She was still thinking about what had occurred the night before. She came to him in despair, only to be devastated. She understood precisely why she was mad, at him and at herself. He was not hers, yet she couldn't imagine letting him go.

She was aware that everything in her head was unreasonable. Her dread of losing him when he was never hers, her rage that threatened to erupt at him when she had no right, everything she felt for him at the time, which sprang from love, was illogical, and she despised it all.

"How are you feeling?" He asked quietly. She didn't respond. She knew that if she opened her lips, only poison would spill out. He said nothing else. They sat there in quiet, fighting in their heads till the day was as brilliant as the sun.

A knock on the door interrupted their line of thinking. Cedric unlocked the door, allowing his butler to enter and serve a magnificent breakfast.

"My Lord, my Lady," he said, "There was a carriage waiting outside the estate the entire night." Evelina's heart fell, panic grabbing her as memories of last night in her study flashed before her eyes. She grasped the blankets firmly. Cedric got a gloomy sensation. He cursed himself once again.

"We brought the driver in. He said that he is her Ladyship's driver." He proceeded. Evelina relaxed noticeably, letting out a long breath. She neglected to send her driver away last night, and it seemed to be working to her benefit. She should return home since she could not remain here much longer. She didn't even lift her head to look at his face, knowing she'd lose control and let everything in her heart erupt. But she had to bear in mind that he meant nothing to her. He was her father's adversary, and she meant nothing to him.

"Thank you," she said out. "Please ask him to get ready to leave." Evelina got out of bed and made her way to the door to go. Her head remained down, her gaze away from his.

"I have asked to send your driver away," he continued after a little pause.

"I need to go home. My parents will be concerned," she said monotonously. Her words struck him in the stomach.

"Your parents have not returned to London yet," he said. Evelina glared up at him. He took a step back when he saw the rage in her eyes.

"Are you spying on my family?" She inquired, her jaws tight and her fury suppressed.

"Noo," he answered, somewhat alarmed, "I am not. I'm not eavesdropping on your family or you."

"How do you know my family is out of London?" She inquired, her rage spilling from her lips.

"I," he groaned while sitting on a couch. He seemed exhausted from lack of sleep. He gazed at her with imploring eyes, begging her to understand, but Evelina had long since closed her heart, and all she could see was red. He knew she would not comprehend. She was clouded by rage, and rightfully so.

"I couldn't help it," he admitted defeat. They shared a minute of silence. Evelina made a move for the door.

"Don't go," he begged, "Please. I am sorry," He said, "I couldn't stop myself from learning about you. I couldn't stay away from you. I apologize."

Evelina, in her wrath, understood what he was saying since she had felt the same way up until last night. She was in love until last night, and now she was just a fool in love.

"Why?" She asked impulsively. She'd asked a prohibited inquiry. She was split about whether she wanted him to respond or not since it would affect everything between them. Her heart yearned for him to speak those three naughty words, but her head knew they would mingle like poison and eventually kill her. The words were on the tip of Cedric's tongue. The words she wanted to hear and he wanted to say aloud.

"I," He answered. Evelina braced herself.

"I don't know," he said instead. Evelina breathed a sigh of relief and sat down on the bed, her back to him. She was startled at herself and didn't comprehend herself. She wanted to hear something different, but when he said something else, it removed a weight from her heart. They knew what was in each other's hearts. They realized they couldn't get what they desired. It was better to live in an illusion than to share their hearts with one other, knowing full well that it would only lead to grief.

Evelina's rage gradually gave way to melancholy. She still wanted to know who that lady was last night, but it wasn't her place to inquire.

"What about breakfast, my Lord? I am hungry," she remarked with a sorrowful heart. He closed his eyes hard as she spoke. She accepted their destiny and let him go; it was now his time to genuinely let her go. But he couldn't make himself do it. He desired one final opportunity to protest their destiny.

"The woman you saw last night," he said.

"I don't want to hear it," she stopped him.

"She was my mistress," he said.

"I said I don't want to hear it," she said, tears in her eyes.

"I hadn't visited her in a long time. I wrote a message dismissing her, and she came to woo me last night," he said, loathing himself even more.

"You are hurting me," she remarked through tears.

"I was sleeping when she came," he said, his words hurting his own heart. "Nothing occurred between us. I agreed to give her compensation and let her keep the estate until she found a new boyfriend. She didn't touch me, and I didn't allow her close to me."

"Stop," she sobbed, burying her face in her hands. Cedric sat on the floor in front of her.

"Evelina," He said softly, "Please forgive me." He gingerly caressed her hands, unsure if he should be in her company. Evelina realized destiny was teasing her, but she couldn't do anything. She smiled as she gazed at him through watery eyes. Cedric dropped his head low in shame, tears welling in his eyes. She pressed a delicate kiss to his forehead. They grasped each other's hands firmly.

A knock on his door had both of them running away from each other, wiping away their tears.

"Enter," Cedric instructed.

"My Lord," His footmen said out of breath.

"What is wrong?" Cedric inquired, alert.

"It's Lady Hannah," he muttered under his breath. "Lord Percival is in the King's council; we can't reach him."

"Where are mother and father?" He inquired worriedly.

"They left for Raymond yesterday," he said. "Neither Lord Octavian nor Lord Dom can be located. Please hurry to the Whitworth manor."

"Ready my carriage, and send for the doctor at once," he told them.

Cedric returned to Evelina as soon as they were alone. He grabbed her face in his hands.

"Please wait for me," he said.

"No," Evelina said, "I am coming with you."

"Evelina, I can't take you to Whitworth manor in this attire," Cedric remarked firmly.

"Give me your tailcoat. I believe someone in your estate will have pants in my size," she remarked, thinking quickly.

"Evelina," Cedric replied, prompting Evelina to narrow her eyes. "I will ask to find clothes for you right away," He murmured, gulping, making her grin.

Cedric felt peaceful. Even if he couldn't have her in his life, he wouldn't let anyone else take his heart.

He could gladly let her go with his heart.

Chapter Eighteen

"What's wrong with Lady Hannah? I read in the ledger that she was in the family's way," Evelina inquired as they drove to Whitworth Manor.

"I am not certain either," Cedric responded calmly, despite the fact that concern was threatening to muddle his head. He needed to retain his composure. The first thing he must do is check on Hannah and then rescue his elder brother from the jaws of hell, if possible.

"Don't worry," Evelina whispered, resting her hand on his. "Everything will be fine." Cedric gazed at her intently. She was dressed in her usual attire, his tailcoat too large for her. Her blazing red hair was tucked carelessly inside his large hat. Her eyes glowed with the knowledge that she would be at his side. He held her hand in his, grateful for her.

In the Arms of a Rake Series

She came to him yesterday, desperate and scared. He hoped he didn't have to visit Whitworth Manor. He wanted to wrap her in his arms and take away everything that made her sad. He wanted her to tell him what had occurred, to confide in him, to entrust him with her secrets. He threatened to annihilate everyone who dared to think negatively of her.

He bemoaned his unfortunate situation. He had to let go of the lady who had put all of her concerns and anxieties in the back of her mind while worrying about him. Will anybody ever adore him like this? Would he accept someone else's love like this? Probably not.

When they arrived at Whitworth Manor, there was commotion everywhere. Evelina followed Cedric inside; it was her first time at Whitworth Manor. Despite being wealthy and powerful, Whitworth never held any soirees or balls at Whitworth Manor. Only the closest of their families and friends were permitted here. She was astounded by the beauty of the setting. It was no less than a royal palace, yet along with the opulence, there was a sense of belonging that made you feel comfortable and at ease. It was so tempting that Evelina forgot why they had come to the estate in the first place.

She looked around and realized that all of the maids and servicemen were standing nervously in the alcoves and near the stairs. Evelina observed the butler reaching for Cedric quickly.

"My Lord," He said, breathing hard, "Lady Hannah has gone into labour. The midwife has been summoned, and they are now in her bedchamber. I dispatched the footmen to the palace to alert Lord Percival, but it seems they are having trouble. I've also sent a message to Raymond, his Lordship."

"Why did everyone leave her alone when she was going to go into labour?" Cedric let out a bark.

"Er, my Lord," the butler said cautiously. "She is only in her seventh month."

"What does that have to do!" Cedric felt a squeeze on his arm before he could finish his statement. He stared back at Evelina, astonished.

"It is unusual to have labor in the seventh month of pregnancy. It may have an impact on both the child's and the mother's health. Stop asking inquiries to your butler; you're making him uncomfortable," she said. Cedric turned to face his butler, who was squirming and evidently uncomfortable.

"Have you called the doctor?" Cedric inquired.

"My Lord, the midwife is present," he said.

"The doctor," Cedric said, "Call the doctor immediately."

Cedric made his way up the stairs to Hannah's room but was halted once again by his butler.

"My Lord," he gasped.

"I'll stand outside until my brother gets back," he said dismissively, and Evelina followed him. They could hear faint cries approaching, which prompted them to accelerate their speed. They gathered in front of the door where Hannah was. Her agonizing cries resonated across the hallway. Cedric automatically stretched out to touch Evelina's hand, and she smiled as she clutched his hand warmly.

The shouts were like pain for Cedric. Maybe he shouldn't have come here without thinking.

"It is alright, my Lord," Evelina said as she leaned toward him. "Every woman goes through this pain while giving birth, though it really makes me never want to have children myself."

"I am sorry," he muttered. Evelina merely gripped his hand harder, saddened that women had to go through this suffering to bring life into the world. He had no idea he could love his mother that much, and now that love was accompanied by humility. A last scream rang out, and a few seconds later, the infant's screams filled the room and reached where they stood. Cedric let out a sigh of relief.

"Congratulations on becoming an uncle, my Lord," Evelina said cheekily. Both of them gazed at one other; Evelina had never seen Cedric with such a large grin on his face, and she giggled to herself, becoming even more in love.

"My Lord," someone murmured, jolting them out of their tiny world. Cedric saw the midwife's expression and knew something was awry. She was pale as a ghost, and he was alarmed.

"May we see the child?" Evelina inquired brightly.

"It's a bad omen. You should stay away, my Lord," Midwife said to Cedric, disregarding Evelina. "It is a bad omen."

Cedric's heart fell. Something awful had occurred. However, the words "what went wrong" remained caught in his throat. He had spent very little time with his brother and sister-in-law. He loathed their connection, he disliked her, but with time he appreciated Hannah as a lady, and he was thankful to Hannah for making his brother the happiest person in the world. He envied their affection and desired it for himself. He was looking forward to his brother's child being born and being an uncle.

"What happened?" Evelina inquired severely, "Is her Ladyship okay? Is the youngster okay?

"My Lord, you should be gone from here. It's a horrible sign," the Midwife said again, dismissing Evelina once again.

"Answer her," Cedric said, making the midwife tremble in terror.

"It's, it's" She murmured. Evelina pulled her aside and made her way to the room, pushing the door wide as the midwife shouted.

"Twins. It's the twins. She gave birth to a dreadful omen. The twins are a bad omen," Midwife said as she followed after them.

Evelina went inside, and Cedric soon followed her. Hannah lay on the bed, weeping her heart out for her children.

"Please do not take my children away," she cried. Evelina got up once. She took up the baby from the crib and put it in Hannah's arms before returning to pick up the second baby and placing it next to her. Cedric remained motionless at the entrance, rage boiling within him. The servants stood about, quietly watching Hannah cry for her children.

"Out!" he hissed menacingly; his tone low.

"Cedric," Evelina snarled. Cedric recognized his voice had startled not only the people standing around him, but also Hannah, and he calmed down his fury.

"Everyone get out," he murmured, suppressing his rage. "And drag Percival back to the manor if necessary."

Everyone dashed out of the chamber in an instant. Cedric made his way toward Evelina. She was the only one unmoved by his rage.

"Please," Hannah screamed again, tears streaming down her cheeks, "Don't take away my children."

"I won't," Cedric said instantly. "And I won't let anyone touch even the single strand of hair on their head, I promise." Evelina assisted Hannah in arranging her infants side by side. Hannah held them and wept quietly. Evelina was smiling at them and toying with the baby's finger, hoping to get them to grasp her finger.

"It's a boy and a girl," Evelina exclaimed, delighted as she looked at Cedric. He rang the doorbell, and the butler entered the room.

"My Lord, my Lady," he bowed.

"Pay compensation to the midwife and ask her to leave," Cedric instructed. "And make clear to everyone before leaving that if anyone dares to speak ill about my niece and nephew, they will answer to me. Tell them not to forget they are the Whitworth heir."

19

Chapter Nineteen

Cedric and Evelina remained in Hannah's chamber until Percival came. They had to keep the doctor waiting since Hannah would not let anybody approach her infants. The doctor couldn't do his examination on Cedric and Evelina in male clothes in the mother's room unless her husband was there. Cedric didn't have the heart to abandon the new parents until more of his family members were around to properly care for them. He was on edge around everyone. Midwife's words lingered in his mind, and he would not accept anybody speaking poorly of his family. Evelina was unsure if she could return home or how long she would have to wait. She sent a message to her estate. She needed to make a plausible justification for her fiancé to avoid raising more suspicion.

In the Arms of a Rake Series

She was served lunch and left alone in the parlor for most of the time. She was growing bored sitting alone, uncertain where Cedric had gone. She was soon escorted to a tiny private library, where Cedric had requested her to wait.

Evelina spent the remainder of the day reviewing the research. She understood it was his own study and felt a rush of excitement. It was intimate and wonderful to be in an area that was special to him. She felt closer to him, butterflies in her stomach, and a brilliant grin spread over her face. She was buzzing with enthusiasm. She attempted to remember a list of all the books he had worn out by reading them again and over. She was shocked to discover the library ever so clean and tidy.

Cedric Whitworth had one whole wall covered with carelessly crammed written notebooks and paper. She grinned to herself and delicately touched the edges of the parchments that were jutting out. In the corner, one sheet stood out more than the rest. Curiosity got the better of her, and she attempted to see what was written on it, which appeared in her hand as soon as she touched it. She attempted to put it back in as gently as she had previously, afraid of being caught prying around.

The phrases on the paper drew her attention, and as she looked it up in the light, her face became pale. It was the first page of the identical paper she had studied in his office: the noblewomen's inheritance law. She now understood why Lord Adam hadn't found anything in his office. The memory of the previous night sent shivers down her spine, and it was too late when she observed the shadow projected on the paper.

She quickly whirled around to see him leaning close to her, with just a hairbreadth separating them. Her breathing was laboured, and her heart thumped hard in her chest.

He approached gently, and she backed backward, only to be halted by his study table. When his lips approached her, she automatically closed her eyes.

"Don't tell me you are snooping through my study too?" He said. She opened her eyes to find herself standing on tiptoes, the sheet ripped from her grasp as he attempted to peek through it. He duped her into believing he was going to kiss her; nevertheless, she was the one who expected him to kiss her.

"You asked me to wait here and it was lying around, if I was not supposed to look at it, you should have kept it safe," she said with a grin.

"Pardon me for the mess, my Lady," He smirked and said, "But why are you so annoyed?"

"I am not annoyed," she said. He returned the parchment to its original location and approached her. She grabbed her pants hard, refusing to flinch at his near closeness. She looked away from him, sulking. She will not let him fool her any longer.

"Were you disappointed I didn't kiss you?" He muttered quietly near her ears, causing electric shocks. She laughed uncomfortably.

"Who even wants to be kissed by you?" She remarked, her voice trembling. He turned her face back to him and looked into her eyes.

"Weren't you the one demanding me to kiss you?" He inquired mischievously.

"I would have lost my mind to demand such a thing, but now I am all sane my Lord," she answered courageously, staring into his eyes, returning to her confident self.

"Are you now?" He whispered again. She placed her hands on his chest, softly pushing him away, knowing the danger that his whispered words and seductive ebony eyes represented.

"Yes, my Lord," she muttered.

Cedric held her hands softly, sliding them to the back of his neck and slowly making her swallow. He wrapped his hands around her waist, narrowing the distance between them. He smirked, and Evelina understood he had duped her again, but before she could object, his lips were on hers, making her forget everything.

They had no idea how long they had been in one other's arms, tracing their lips over one another's skin. Evelina was now seated on the desk, her legs securely wrapped over his head. Despite their refusal to let each other go, they were hesitant to go any farther in a study where anybody might enter at any moment.

True to their worries, a footman promptly knocked on the door to inform Cedric that his parents had returned. He requested that a guest room be prepared for Evelina and that supper be given to her immediately, much to her displeasure.

"Sorry, my Lady," Cedric murmured, adjusting both of their garments. "My mother has very sharp eyes. She will recognize that you are not a man with just one glance. Now, unless you wish to tell the whole truth, it is best if you avoid her gaze since nothing escapes her."

"I was thinking about going back home," she murmured gently.

"No," he insisted, "Not tonight."

He calmed himself down and grasped her hand, attempting to exhibit a plaintive expression that only made him seem intimidating. Evelina laughed at his antics.

"Please wait for me," His face may have failed, but his words revealed every feeling. Evelina raised her toes and kissed him on the cheeks.

"Don't keep me waiting for too long, my Lord," she whispered, faltering away from him.

The footman was waiting outside to transport her to the guest room. She waited in her room for a long time, still wearing her waistcoat and pants, and then fell asleep. She awoke in the middle of the night to find him looking fondly at her and touching her hair.

"What do you want me to do?" He said, noting she had awoken, "You can ask for anything from me, and I will do it."

"Is that a promise, my Lord?" She asked.

"No," he said. "Promises may be broken. But this is more than a promise; I will fulfill everything you want for."

"Then I do have something to ask of you?" She said, cuddling up to him. Silence, with just the sound of their breathing and the crackling of the fire.

"I am ready, my Lady," Cedric said after a few minutes. "Ask it."

If Evelina had ordered him to rend his chest open and offer his heart, he would have done so, and she was aware of it. She could have asked him to marry her, and he would have consented immediately. She wanted so much from him, yet she could only ask for so little.

"That stuffed parchment in your study," she continued. "Place it in our constitution."

20

Chapter Twenty

They were struggling to keep their eyes open due to weariness from the previous day. They yearned for every single second to extend into eternity. The pleasant stillness was lulling them to sleep, but all they wanted to do was soak in each other's presence for as long as possible. They needed a talk to get them through the night, a reason to embrace one another till daybreak. They will say their goodbyes in the morning, but first, they want to experience their whole existence in one night.

"Evelina," Cedric muttered.

"Evelina, my Lord," Evelina replied exhaustedly. "My name is Evelina."

"That's why I will always call you Evelina because you will never let anyone call you by anything else," he replied with a smile.

"What makes you think I will let you call me Evelina?" She inquired with a raised eyebrow.

"Aren't you already letting me do it?" He remarked cheekily.

"You are infuriating," she said.

"Only to you," he said.

Silence filled the holes in the night, and it was as comforting as when the words were uttered.

"Evelina," he said once more.

"Yes, Will," she said, making him stare at her.

"Do not call me that," he replied, partially sitting and looming over her.

"How about Willy?" She inquired with feigned innocence.

"Not!" He screamed.

"I guess I am going to Domname you, Willy," she added honestly, "Or maybe Will. I haven't decided yet."

"No, you're not going to call me anything except Cedric. I forbid it," He said.

"We will see about that," She said, "Will," mumbling it weakly.

They remained in one another's arms, and once again, sleep was a beautiful temptation attempting to separate them.

"What happened that day?" Cedric asked, squeezing his fist. He steeled his emotions, knowing that the response he got would not be one he could hear. Evelina shuddered at his inquiry, as images of the night rushed through her head. He drew her closer, inhaling the aroma of her hair and showing her that he was now with her. Evelina let out a long breath. She didn't want to spoil the great night, but she also wanted to pour her heart out to him. But talking about it, even with the person she felt most at ease with, was a herculean feat; the word wouldn't escape her lips.

There was only one way she could tell him without reliving those terrifying moments and transforming them into something foreign, soulless. She braced herself, unsure whether she could get through this.

"I kicked my fiancé," she laughed, "At his manhood."

Cedric gazed at her with wide-open eyes, as if he sensed her suffering, and immediately pulled his manhood away from her slightly. Her laughter filled the room.

"Pardon my reaction, Evelina," He apologized, "I am certain Lord Vaughn must have deserved it."

"He, uh," Evelina attempted to continue, but the words were trapped in her throat, "I." Cedric hugged her closely once more, and she tucked her head in his chest, listening to his pulse to calm herself down.

"I'm his fiancée. As my future husband, he has the right to demand wife duties from me, but I couldn't and he was drunk," she muttered, causing Cedric to tighten his grip on her.

"He is treating my house as if it is already his. He speaks as if my father's duchy would be his once we marry, and he treats my staff like they are his own. I despise him. He's absolutely disgusting," she murmured between her tears. When her sob stopped, Cedric was enraged.

He intended to assassinate Lord Vaughn, but Evelina's next question pulled him back to reality.

"Do you think it was wrong of me to deny his rights as a future husband?" She inquired with tremendous discomfort.

"No," Cedric said honestly. "Never." Silence. Absolute quiet caused her to hiccup like a sledgehammer to his heart.

"I have never thought of this before," he added hesitantly. "It was okay to me for a woman to execute her responsibilities as her husband required. I was prepared to demand an heir from my future bride, and now that this has happened to you, I despise myself for the man I was."

"Perhaps I was mistaken. I am not sure what ladies require. I was so focused on the noblewomen receiving their estates that I failed to analyze my own failings. I believed I would be doing a tremendous favour to ladies by supplying them with this one. I don't even know what women need the most," he remarked, distraught.

"We can ask them," Evelina replied, rubbing his hair to relax him.

"Who? How many?" He stated he was troubled.

"All of them," she said, smiling.

"Yes, let's do that," he replied, inhaling her aroma.

"I think what you are doing is something we need but we simply don't understand it till we are put in the position of loss," she added after a moment of quiet.

"What made you think that, my Lady?" Cedric inquired.

"I am concerned that my inept fiancée will become the master of my house after my marriage. I'd rather burn down the estate with my own hands than let him flee like it was his bloody stable house," she added, angry.

"You were trying to make me understand it all along," she replied, her gaze distant.

"Forgive me," He murmured. "I never intended for you to interpret it in this way. I can't desire for you to have lived in the same world you used to live in, but I wish you could have understood this grief in a different manner, rather than when it was poured on you."

"No, my Lord," Evelina said, "I should thank you. I'm one of those ladies who needs you to fight for them. That stuffed parchment in your study may be our salvation."

"Evelina," Cedric answered. "Please do not marry him."

He wanted to say something, but suddenly he was ready to marry her. He would not even consider such ideas since he knows they would lead him down the road of impossible. In the end, she was his adversary's daughter. He couldn't listen to his emotions since too much was at risk. His love was a little cost for his goal and family.

"Will you convey my gratitude to your mother?" She asked: "She shaped you into the man you are; even if you started working on the inheritance bill for your mother, you want it to benefit everyone. I never imagined that a lady like me could possess an estate just for the sake of saving her life."

"I will," he answered gently. "I also need to seek her forgiveness. I made her vision my dream, only to abandon it when it proved ineffective. I failed to be the son my mother had raised me to be."

"We can strive to be better," she remarked.

"We should always strive to be better," he remarked. The remainder of the night was spent with a heavy anguish in both of their hearts, and the sense of helplessness turned into a burning desire to do something, to change something.

With the same fire in their hearts, they parted ways in the morning to fight their own battles.

21

Chapter Twenty-one

When lovers split, they either evaporate into oblivion or the world witnesses a reckoning like never before. They may either numb themselves or channel all they have into bravery. Cedric and Evelina chose the latter. Both of their battlefields were completely different; Evelina stood in front of her parents, while Cedric was in front of his whole party, but for both of them, everything was on the line.

Evelina's parents have always shown her a lot of affection. Even though she was rebellious and disregarded the standards, she had never opposed her parents. Apart from her unmarried status, her parents have never been disappointed in her. She had never hesitated before. But here she was, standing in front of her parents, who had never turned her down

In the Arms of a Rake Series

for anything. As far as she recalls, she has always been crude and uncultured, never the noblewoman she should have been, yet her parents never said a word of criticism. Her parents let her do anything she pleased; she was as free as a bird.

She nearly took a step back and walked back the way she had come. Her bravery weakened in front of her family, who had only shown her love and acceptance. It was quite difficult to stand against folks who had never done anything wrong. They never asked her to marry Lord Vaughn, either. Lord Vaughn discovered her snooping and covert rendezvous with Cedric due to her ignorance. He just blackmailed her parents, and they did not ask her for anything. If she had not accepted Lord Adam's marriage proposal, her parents would have handled the situation differently.

Evelina could only recall all the horrible things she had done. The shame was attempting to swallow her whole. If she goes against her parents now, won't she be the worst daughter ever? Is this how she planned to thank them for their unwavering love? Evelina couldn't make herself do it. She would sooner suffer all her life than defy her parents.

"Evy," her father's concerned voice reached her ears. His palm massaged her shoulder, relaxing her. "What is the matter, my darling daughter?" He inquired, sitting with his wife in front of their disturbed daughter.

"I have something to ask both of you," she said nervously.

"Darling," her mother asked her father. "Are you certain this is our daughter?"

"Mother," she complained, making her parents giggle. Evelina was relieved since the air was no longer stuffy.

"What if someone has never done anything wrong but what seemed right to them didn't harm anyone till now," She attempted to construct her inquiry as she spoke since she was never the kind to plan ahead of time.

"Is it harming someone now?" Her father asked.

"I am not certain but it feels wrong," she remarked.

"If anything seems wrong, it's possible that it is, and they should look into it more. It is always preferable to obtain information, and even if everything your instinct tells you is incorrect, sometimes it is better to follow your own gut than all the knowledge in the world," her father remarked.

"Father," Evelina remarked, comforted by her father's comments, "Who is the heir to our Duchy?" The quiver in her parents' faces confirmed her biggest dread.

"You know it, darling," her mother said. "Why such a sudden question?"

"Did you promise Lord Vaughn our duchy?" She asked fearlessly.

"Darling," her mother replied, worriedly.

"Yes," her father said, "We don't have many options left. He has more than enough to demolish every piece of honour our forefathers have toiled for throughout the years."

"I am sorry," Evelina replied, her head down.

"This is not your fault. We were too gentle with you, but we couldn't have been harder if we tried." He groaned.

In the Arms of a Rake Series

"You can't give our duchy to Lord Vaughn," she said with pleasure.

"It is for your own good now that you are to be married," Her mother said, "Your children will inherit the duchy in the future."

"Why can't I inherit the duchy?" She inquired enthusiastically.

"What do you mean?" Her father inquired skeptically.

"Lord Vaughn wants the Duchy of Winchester. Will inheriting the duchy fulfill the objective after we marry?" She asked.

"That is ridiculous," her mother said. "You cannot inherit the duchy, darling. You are not the Lord. The law prohibits a woman from owning property.

"I assumed you would advocate for your cousin to inherit the duchy rather than your betrothed. Who convinced you that you could?" Her father asked.

"You only have one daughter, why didn't you ever think of using your power to introduce a bill that can allow your daughter, your only heir to inherit what is rightfully hers?" She asked, annoyed.

"Evelina," her mother remarked angrily. "Is this how you speak to your father?"

"Evy, what is wrong with you?" Her father inquired, "You never showed any interest in the duchy before."

"I was a child, and I was naive and foolish," She muttered, "How could I have known I wouldn't be that carefree my whole life? Did you not believe it was vital to educate me about the world, even if as a girl I was simply married off to someone? If I had been a man, would you have been more concerned with my maturation?"

Evelina felt defeated. The study had become eerily quiet. Tears welled in her eyes, and she rose up and walked away, not daring to look at her parents. Had she crossed the line? Perhaps she should go back and apologize.

"Cedric Whitworth," her father's voice reached her, stopping her movements at the entrance. "He is the one who filled your head with this garbage, didn't he?"

"He has nothing to do with this, father," Evelina said. "And would that be so bad? For him to remind me that I should be concerned about my future, my parents, my duchy, and my people. To convince me that I might be something greater, something different."

As the words flowed out of her, she understood he was the one who believed in her even when she did not.

"For goodness' sake, he's the reason everything is a bloody mess," her mother said.

"It is not, Mother," Evelina said quietly. "I was the one who did badly, and I do not regret it. I wish certain things were different, but..."

"Do you fancy him?" Her father asked bluntly.

Evelina's head snapped up towards her father. She could not believe what her father had asked her. Her heart pounded hard in her chest. A glimmer of hope appeared: would he, maybe he would. No, would there be any possibility that if she liked him, they could be together? Every star in heaven knew she wanted to be with him, and each second without him was a slow death. Her parents gazed at each other, and when they glanced back at her with words more lethal than poison, she wished she had never been.

"Cedric Whitworth was the one who paid the agent in the Ledger to publish your Library escapade," her father remarked with a smirk.

"N-no," Evelina moaned.

"You think I would have simply agreed to Lord Vaughn because he found you with Cedric Whitworth in parliament," her father continued. "I accepted his condition because I needed to stop him from investigating further. If he ever discovers that Cedric Whitworth began all of this, he will drag your name through the dirt, and we will have lost everything. I rather have you marry Lord Vaughn than linked with that Whitworth."

22

Chapter Twenty-two

Evy's heart had been broken, which filled her with rage. She was convinced that if she ever met Cedric Whitworth, she would murder him with her own hands. He humiliated her, but she couldn't bring herself to hate him. But there was a lot of hatred directed at her. She couldn't believe what had happened. He was supposed to be her knight in shining armour, not the one who stabs her in the back.

Everything that happened between them felt manufactured. She believed she could read Cedric Whitworth like an open book, but she was duped. She danced on his fingertips all along, dreaming of a beautiful future, happy in the knowledge that he wanted the same thing somewhere in his heart, but all of her dreams were dashed.

She hoped it was a nightmare and that she would wake up soon. She lay on her bed, staring at the ceiling, feeling her energy drain away. It was an unsettling feeling because she was never the type to sit idle and do nothing, but here she was, avoiding life.

Her wedding preparations had begun in earnest days ago. She hadn't left her chamber in a long time, having withdrawn into her world of despair and suffering. Her wedding date had been set, and now all she had to do was walk down the aisle, marry the man she despises, and spend the rest of her life locked up in another cage.

Her mother had come to request that she prepare for the ball. Even though it was widely reported in the newspapers that she was marrying Lord Vaughn, the couple had yet to attend a ball together. Evelina wanted to refuse, but her mother's worried expression made her swallow her emotions and get ready for the ball.

Lord Vaughn arrived late to meet his future wife. Evelina stood next to her parents, silently accepting the congratulations and spreading lies about her fiancé's whereabouts. She had no idea where he was instead of being here with her, but she didn't care. She knew who else wouldn't be present: the man she still desired.

Even just thinking about his name made her stomach turn. She should be furious at him. He did a terrible thing to her and then lied about her, calling her a fool, but the heart wants what it wants. She wanted him to approach her and tell her that he wasn't to blame and that her parents were mistaken. Was it too much to ask him to come forward just to laugh at her for being the fool he always knew she was?

"Lord Whitworth," her father's voice echoed in her ears. She looked up to see an elderly couple in front of them: the Lord and Lady of Whitworth, Whitworth children's parents. She now knew where Cedric got his onyx eyes; they were identical to his father's ocean of pitch-black darkness.

"Lord Winchester," Lord Whitworth replied, "Many congratulations on your daughter's upcoming nuptials."

"Yes, thank you," Her father said calmly. "Many congratulations on the birth of your grandchildren."

The interaction between the couple was so bland. Their families were on opposite ends, and they made no effort to overcome their indifference. They mostly just greeted each other at balls, but Evelina was never present to witness the conversation.

"Thank you very much, my Lord, my Lady," Lady Whitworth exclaimed enthusiastically.

"When is the christening?" Her mother's request was in vain. Evelina wished the charade would end soon. She is unable to bear the formalities between their families. She couldn't understand why they needed to go through this.

"Two days later at Westminster," she responded, "I should be home going over all the preparation than being here."

In the Arms of a Rake Series

"Darling, everything is completed." Lord Whitworth told his wife, "You should relax," and they left the Winchester's.

Evelina watched as the older couple walked to the dance floor. She turned her gaze back to her parents. The harsh reality hit her in the face. She had always assumed that her parents loved each other, but after closely watching the Whitworth couple, she realized that her parents' love paled in comparison. She frantically looked around the ballroom, her gaze moving from one couple to the next, determining who was in love and who was not. Her head started spinning, and her breathing became laboured.

"Evy, Evy," her parents faintly called out to her. Darkness took over. When she awoke, she was in her bedroom. Her worried parents looked at her, and the woman beside her tested her nerves. She wasn't a doctor, and she'd never heard of any female doctors in the United Kingdom or anywhere else. Evelina attempted to sit up, but the woman warned her not to move.

She stood still until the woman prodded her here and there.

"You do not need to be afraid," the woman said, "She simply lacks energy. Make her eat a lot and cut back on the wedding planning." The woman's appearance speaks louder than her words. Who was she, anyway? And why did her parents bring her rather than a doctor? Was she even qualified to tell us what was wrong with her?

"Thank you for your service," her father said, "You will receive your payments soon." She exited the chamber without saying anything or giving a backward glance. Her father summoned the butler and requested that he take her to the doctor right away.

"What is going on? Who was that woman?" Evelina had numerous questions.

"First, you will eat your food, and I will watch you until you eat every last bit of it," her mother said, calling for the maid to bring her food. Her parents remained silent as she sipped the hot soup. The doctor arrived quickly and performed some routine checkups.

"No need to worry, my Lady," he told Evelina. "You appear to be simply exhausted from wedding preparation. This is requested of me at every house with a bride-to-be present. I understand that your wedding will only happen once in your life, but do not ignore eating at the proper times and getting enough rest."

Evelina's displeasure with the doctor was obvious on her face. The doctor quickly realized what he was doing and stopped talking. He assured her parents of her health once more before leaving

"Make sure she is properly taken care of," her father replied. "I will be back in three days. Her father massaged Evelina's head and kissed her mother's forehead.

"Where are you going, father?" She inquired in a low voice.

"Your father has to visit Winchester for a few days," her mother said

"I will be back before you know it," her father remarked, leaving the mother and daughter alone

"Why so suddenly?" Evelina questioned her mother

"We don't need to meddle in men's affairs," her mother said simply. Evelina despised it. She wanted to yell, complain, and beg, but she resisted.

"Then let us discuss about women's issues. Who was the woman? And why was she here?" Evelina inquired, furious.

"She was simply here to confirm our doubts," her mother said faintly.

"What doubts?" Evelina inquired curiously. Her mother stared at her directly.

"We wanted to know if you are with a child."

23

Chapter Twenty-three

Cedric was no longer bothered by the commotion surrounding him. Except for the two sunshines, everything was the same: dark and nothingness. He was scheduled to be godfather today. With tremendous difficulty, he summoned the energy to conceal his sad self, which would vanish briefly. His ego, which believed that nothing could hurt him, had burst into flame. He maintained his attention exclusively on the twins. He was using them as a barrier, hoping that their faces would distract him from his terrible thoughts, and they did.

After the ceremony, they returned to the mansion, where his family had hosted lavish dinners for all of London's upper-class nobles, including the Queen and Prince. Cedric made it a point to visit every prominent guest at the feast, and he accidentally stopped by the circle discussing about Winchester. He attempted to eavesdrop, but there was no point since so many people had come to hear what others had to say. Cedric stood there, listening to the discussion.

"It was strange," A woman stood up and said, "For Lady Winchester to faint in the ball like that and then her family refusing to call for the doctor but insisting on taking her home." Cedric's heart was filled with anxiety, so he resolved to go see Evelina and check on her right away. His soul will not rest until he has seen her for himself. But the following word made him stand straight in his place.

"I know that 8 out of 10 cases of fainting or falling ill before their wedding are due to exhaustion from the preparations, but the remaining two are getting married because they fainted first," someone said, eliciting a scornful laugh from others. Cedric balled his fist and longed to slam it into the faces of everybody who spoke ill of her.

"Do you think Lady Winchester comes in those 2?" Someone asked.

"Well, her parents' behaviour was certainly saying there was more under the hood than her exhaustion," Someone came in and said, "And who would want to marry such an unrefined lady anyway, she has to use other means to catch herself a husband." Cedric stood there listening to them, the words hardly registering in his head. All of their talk led to Evelina's pregnancy, which might be his child. His gaze shifted to the twins who were the focus of attention today, and he realized he wasn't prepared to be a parent. He wanted to offer his children the world, but he was not willing to sacrifice all for them.

Everything around Cedric grew silent; his mind could no longer perceive anything. Then they couldn't be considered his offspring. She might just be using him. The message he discovered a few days earlier made things more obvious for him. He chose to maintain his distance from Evelina, despite his heart's strong protests. He shut off his thinking and stepped away from the mob.

Even though he decided to avoid her, and even if evidence indicated that she was his adversary, he couldn't bring himself to detest her. He wishes she weren't with a child. He had no idea what to do if the child was his, or how to continue his life knowing that the lady he loved was carrying someone else's child. Everything made him furious.

Cedric felt weary. He hasn't been sleeping well for some days. He can't seem to control the erratic ideas that raced through his mind. Despite the fact that the celebration was still going on, he decided to retire for the day. He shared his ideas with his mother, who advised he take a sabbatical. She didn't want his absence to spark further rumors. Cedric sat down in his office room and opened the hidden drawer, which now contained just one document with Evelina's handwriting.

Every time he looks at those words, his mind searches for another answer, one that does not involve breaching his trust. But then his cautious side reminds him of who she is, and the letter is evidence she deceived him. Cedric clutched the paper in his hand and tossed his head back on the sofa. He saw a lady waiting at the entrance, and his face brightened up at the thought of seeing Evelina again. But she was not Evelina.

"My Lord," She added, "I hope I'm not bothering you. I was worried because you left the celebration so early."

"Lady Vernon," Cedric said to his betrothed. "Please take a seat. I came to get some rest. Would you want some brandy?"

"No, thank you, my Lord," She sat in front of him and remarked, "I do not do well with alcohol." Evelina might compete with him in drinking, and maybe even defeat him. He dismissed the notion as soon as it entered his thoughts.

"Pardon me, I only have alcohol in my office chamber," Cedric remarked with a smile, "I will ring for the footmen right away to bring something for you."

"Thank you, my Lord," she replied with a smile. "I thought being a politician, the crowd like this will be a child's play for you, but you are really nothing like what ton portrays you to be."

"Are you saying I am incapable of being a politician?" He inquired with raised eyebrows. He could see her face blanching. He was aware she was having an affair and ventured to doubt his competence; was he really going to marry someone like her? Perhaps Evelina was correct in her assessment that he should cancel his wedding, but doing so would jeopardize his reputation and job, which is what Evelina may have in mind.

"I am simply trying to understand you, my Lord," Her remarks drew him back from his own thoughts. "I don't believe anybody is competent to doubt your ability, much alone me. I was attempting to understand you better, my Lord; after all, we are getting married very soon. I don't intend to offend you."

"Pardon me, I came here to spend some time alone," he remarked, agitated.

"I will leave you to your devices, my Lord," Standing up, she remarked, "Please do not forget that we have to announce our engagement at tonight's celebration." Cedric totally forgot about the announcement. They never publicly announced their engagement, even though everyone was well aware of it at this point. Cedric cursed his luck. He did not wish to marry Lady Vernon.

"Are you still carrying her?" A high-pitched voice frightened Cedric to the point that he almost fell off the sofa. There stood Evelina in her male disguise, battling with the drapes that refused to let her depart.

"Ah, bloody tarnation," she bemoaned the drapes that kept her feet trapped. Cedric could only stare in a stupor as she unceremoniously released herself from the tangles and made her way to him. She was nothing like a woman, making strange facial expressions, dropping her hat on the floor, and having her hair plastered to her head like a nest.

"What! "What are you doing here?" Cedric murmured so quietly that Evelina didn't hear it.

In the Arms of a Rake Series

"Oh, congratulations on being the godfather," she added with a smile, "The twins are looking so adorable tonight, I wanted to pinch their cheeks so hard.

"How did you get in?" Cedric said in a concerned tone.

"What?"

"How did you enter Whitworth manor?"

"Oh, that's one of my talents," she remarked jokingly.

"You mean the infiltration," he stated accusingly.

"Pardon me," she murmured, realizing there was something amiss. Cedric placed the coiled-up letter from his palm on the table.

"This is your handwriting, isn't it?" He asked. Evelina took up the note that stated: **Whitworth Manor's infiltration was successful. -K**

24

Chapter Twenty-four

Evelina stared at the message with terror. It was intended to be with her parents at her home, not at the Whitworth mansion with Cedric. She now understood why her parents assumed she was with the child since they hadn't received her letter from the night she spent with Cedric at Whitworth Manor.

It was only a mistake; she had a fine explanation for Cedric, but when she glanced up at the man she loved, all she saw was anguish. She was aware of the dreadful ache. She had gone through it herself when her parents informed her that Cedric was the one who had soiled her name in the ledger. She couldn't trust him any more than he trusted her.

The sight in his eyes was the same as the one she saw in the mirror: sadness, suspicion, and a sense of emptiness that no one else could replace. Evelina lost all confidence to talk since she knew he would not believe whatever she said. The words on the message were hers, and he trusted them more than he did her. What was this sense of hopelessness? Was this what defeat felt like? Standing in front of each other, with all the misery they have caused one other, they should be fighting like the worst enemies.

Their hearts would shatter once more. There would be no way out of the agony they had caused one other. She knew the quiet surrounding them had made it plain that this was the end for them, but she still wanted to attempt to find that final thread of hope.

"Cedric," Evelina answered with trepidation.

"Leave," Cedric commanded, breaking no negotiations.

"At the very least, listen to me," Evelina said.

"Leave now," Cedric murmured, unable to look up at her, "I do not want to make a scene by throwing you out of the manor."

"You wouldn't do that," Evelina remarked, frustrated.

"I am asking for the last time, leave now," Cedric said once again, without looking at her. "Don't make me call the guards, Evelina."

"You will not call the guards on me, Cedric Whitworth. You will not cause a disruption in your family celebration that will ruin your family's reputation on tomorrow's ledger," she stated fiercely.

"You should be worried about your own reputation, my Lady," Cedric responded angrily.

"The reputation that you have already ruined," Evelina delivered the ultimate blow. Cedric heard her words correctly, but the quiet that followed was like a hammer to his heart.

"What? What do you mean?" Cedric spoke with his back to her, fearing that she would see the truth on his face.

"Weren't you the one behind my library debacle painted in the ledger?" Evelina inquired. Cedric glanced around a shocked expression on his face. It was like the last beam of sunlight, shining brilliantly before going away in an instant and darkness creeping in.

"How did you find out?" He asked hesitantly.

Evelina didn't accept her parents' words when they informed her that Cedric was the one who began everything, that he was the source of all her pain, and that nothing could hurt her more than that, but she was mistaken once again.

Hearing those words from his mouth, which were an indirect confirmation of her charge, silenced her heart. It felt the same as when she was losing consciousness, but she was fully awake now. She had no idea how she returned to the road she had taken while leaving the Whitworth house. She strolled along the cobblestone street with a blank mind, as if her spirit had abandoned her completely. She didn't know how, but she got to her room.

She lay down on her bed and couldn't recall how she got there. She knew she had recovered her carriage and returned, but she wasn't really present. It seemed like she was entirely lost inside herself.

The days passed in a whirl. She would see everything and do all that was expected of her, but she felt like someone else was moving her body while she remained still. She had lost herself, and what remained was only a shell.

"Why don't you tell her the truth?"

"I feel this is easy and kind," Cedric stated.

"Or cowardly." Cedric had nothing to say about it. It was definitely cowardly. Why didn't he stop her and reveal the truth? He was guilty of the crime she accused him of, but not in the manner she expected. Not in the manner that crushed her heart. And yet he was here, looking for ways to excuse what he had done.

After Evelina departed, he sat in his office for quite some time, looking into nothingness. The pandemonium raced wild within him, his heart screaming for him to follow her and tell her everything, but the letter on his desk stopped him every second. He refused all of his footmen's demands to join the party again. Everyone was waiting for him to announce his engagement to Lady Vernon. He knew he was trying Lord Vernon's patience. If that individual desired, he might put a stop to Cedric's career.

He was astonished to find Hannah on his porch. Before he could stop himself, he told her everything, and she departed, urging him not to leave his office chamber. Nobody came to search for him after that.

He still had no idea what she accomplished, but whatever it was, it kept Cedric's name out of his family's scoldings.

The Vernons wrote him a letter expressing their disappointment but requesting that the announcement be made as soon as his health permitted.

Following the party, his parents and siblings gave him anxious glances but did not approach him. He knew Hannah was assisting him in preventing everyone from pestering him with questions. He had not responded to any summons from the parliament or the Vernons. He ate little and seldom left his bedchamber. He was often visiting the twins, and Hannah had caught him once asking the newborns for guidance. Since that day, they've been sitting in the nursery in quiet. Hannah never spoke about anything. She never asked him questions or offered reassurance. Today she questioned him why he won't give her the truth. He was such a coward, burying himself in his grief.

"It is not cowardly," Cedric responded, trying not to blush in front of her. "I simply believe this is what is best for everyone."

"Cedric, I know what a coward is!" Hannah responded carelessly. Cedric was astonished to discover this brave side of her. "I have been a coward, and I know you are the same," she said honestly.

In the Arms of a Rake Series

"The strange thing about cowards is that they believe they are the bravest. We are doing this for the benefit of everyone. So, what are we doing? We are merely causing suffering for everyone else because we are in agony."

"I believed I was being courageous by leaving Percival since it meant defending Whitworth's reputation and, by extension, the pleasure of everyone around him. I considered myself a strong woman who was willing to sacrifice her own happiness for his, even though I knew he would be unhappy."

"But I never considered the possibility that my happiness may make others happy. My decision to live with Percival will make him happy, which will make everyone else happy as well."

"We gave so much importance to our sacrifice, our pain, our bravado, that we do not see we are not who we think we are." Cedric understood what Hannah said, but comprehension and acceptance were two distinct concepts.

Humans are quite excellent at misleading, and they excel at fooling themselves. What the mind knows but does not embrace is never reflected in its actions, and Cedric was no different. But Hannah's remarks kept gnawing at his insides.

Was he being cowardly?

25

Chapter Twenty-five

No, it cannot be. He had considered every option and was certain that what he was doing was best. But best for whom? Was it best for him? How was it best for him when he spent his days in agony? Knowing he had broken the heart of the lady he really loved and cared about. She certainly hates him now. After all, he didn't clear the air about his role in the library disaster. But she also injured him.

He wasn't sure whether it was destiny or bad luck, but he ordered that any missives leaving the manor on the day of the twins' birth be stopped and brought to him first to ensure that no unpleasant remarks spread. He relied on his family's trusted service providers to keep everyone else in check.

In the Arms of a Rake Series

She was wiser than he gave her credit for. The memo was directed to her father's workplace. A politician receiving an infiltration message might be portrayed in any manner feasible. There was nothing he could prove. But he knew his greatest dread had come true as Evelina's face drained from the realization of the message. She played Cedric like a violin. He realized it was all his fault. He was aware of the implications of fraternizing with the enemy, yet he allowed his emotions get the better of him. And now he is paying the price he never dreamed of.

His footman coughed, pulling him back into reality. He was suited up for the last party he wanted to attend. Evelina was being married the next day, and her family had planned a lavish wedding reception for the couple. Naturally, with all of the aristocracy in London, the invitation was extended to the Whitworths as well. Except for Cedric, no other member of his family had a direct dispute with Winchester. Simply put, their lifestyles were dramatically different. While Winchester's were quite conventional and conservative, Whitworth wanted to challenge the standards and live an adventurous lifestyle.

Hannah was leaving the estate for the first time since the twins' birth, and his parents enthusiastically consented to stay with them. Since his brother's message claimed that they were someplace in Scotland doing God knows what, Cedric had no option but to join the party. He felt cursed. He was at the pre-wedding reception of the lady he loved, who not only crushed his heart but also made a mockery of him. Everyone would laugh at him behind his back.

Her father would have been his opponent, but he was a highly accomplished politician, and to be beaten in such a manner made Cedric ashamed of himself.

He wanted to ask Hannah for a favour so he wouldn't have to attend the party. He waited in the lobby for the couple to come, who were still fretting over their kids. Hannah assured Percival that everything would be ok and that his parents were certainly capable of caring for two newborns after raising four sons. She was clearly angered by his brother; he would need to approach cautiously if he wanted to get his way.

"Hannah," Cedric replied happily, "Why do I feel like you have three children instead of two."

"Hey," Percival said, responding to his brother's remark.

"And I don't want a fourth," Hannah said, narrowing her gaze. Did she already see through him? Even so, it was still worth a chance.

"It has been so long since you had stepped out of the house, Hannah, I think..."

"No," Hannah stopped him in the midst, "You are coming with us, and I will not be fooled by your phony grin. Save it for your parliament."

Hannah went away, and he stared up at his brother in disbelief. The other just smiled at him, rubbed his back, and moved ahead, inviting him to follow. Certainly, Hannah had told Percival everything. Oh, how he despised married people at the time. Would he be like that when he got married? God forbid! He was never going to be that man.

But withholding things from Evelina upset Cedric in ways he hadn't felt before, and all he wanted to do was rush to her and spill his heart out.

"Cedric," Hannah said through the carriage, "I do not want to spend my night in the carriage waiting." His feet twitched in dread of upsetting Hannah anymore.

He was unsure if he or his brother would survive if they did anything to irritate her. Cedric cautiously positioned himself in front of the pair. The travel to Winchester was swift and quiet. He had no idea they lived so close together, or whether it was just his desire to take his time getting to the estate. Cedric saw his fingers trembling uncontrollably. He had never been terrified before, but here he was standing at the door of the lady who had trodden on his heart, and he couldn't help but be thrilled to meet her, speak to her, and hug her.

He wondered whether he could stare at her without expressing his feelings. Will he be able to bear her happiness in someone else's arms? When she looks at him and tells her fiancée how they humiliated him. When his family congratulated them, she accepted with great joy and said that she couldn't wait to marry someone other than him.

A gloved hand gripped his trembling hand strongly. He glanced up to find Percival and Hannah still in the carriage, intently observing him.

"It'll be fine," Hannah responded, shaking his hand. Percival nodded at him, saying the same thing quietly.

"Tell her the truth," she advised. "You deserve it and she deserves it." Cedric was certainly not going to do that. He would be the best version of the stone statue, leaving as quickly as possible. With a sad heart, he moved his steps toward the door. He felt agonizing discomfort with every movement he made. He walked following the back of Percival's head since he lacked the confidence to confront Evelina yet.

His eyes were flooded with dazzling light, and the song tore through his eardrums, causing his head to ache.

Cedric couldn't help but admire the magnificence of the Winchester estate. He had never been there before, yet the grandeur and beauty were breathtaking. It was still situated in the centuries-old stone walls, bringing him on a historical tour. He was reminded that the Winchesters, like the Whitworths, were one of Britain's oldest families. They were only second to the five great families on the King's council.

When Hannah tugged his hand with the point of his sleeves, Cedric's gaze was drawn around the castle walls, soaking in all of its majesty. He saw her gaze fixed in front of him. Cedric followed Hannah's line of view to see Lord Vaughn, with Evelina slightly behind him.

She wasn't how he had anticipated to find her. All of Cedric's fears and judgments vanished like molten lava, and his feet went independently toward the lady he loved. The condition in which he saw Evelina destroyed his determination to avoid her. She wasn't joyful in the arms of another, and she wasn't mocking him behind his back. It was far worse.

She stood there like a living corpse.

26

Chapter Twenty-six

Cedric couldn't bear seeing her. Her face was plastered in more powder than ever before. Her cheekbones were hollow and covered with unappealing fake blush, which obscured her lovely freckles. Her hair was dyed in a deeper tint, making it seem nearly brownish rather than blazing red. Her stance was stooped, as if she was attempting to disguise her height next to her fiancé, and her outfit seemed like it was draped on a slender tree rather than her wearing it since she had become thinner since the last time Cedric saw her.

Cedric moved straight in front of the pair, her bright eyes devoid of all glitter and covered with another layer of powder. Her face contorted into a phony grin, which faded as she recognized Cedric standing there. She glanced aside, attempting to pull her mask up again but failing miserably. "Congratulations on the nuptials, my Lord, my Lady," Percival's voice echoed from one side of Cedric, bringing him back to reality.

"Lord Whitworth," Lord Vaughn said cheerfully, his gaze fixed on Percival while Cedric's was totally on the lady beside him, "I am so glad you could join us for such a happy occasion."

"Lord Cedric, glad you could join us, too," Lord Vaughn replied, turning to Cedric. "Allow me to present you to my betrothed, Lady Evelina Winchester. You must have known her." He remarked mockingly, "After all, her father is the one who is always standing against you in parliament."

Lord Vaughn' comments were not lost on anybody. Everyone knew what he was attempting to convey. Hannah gently drew Cedric away before there could be a full-fledged confrontation. But Hannah was mistaken; he didn't care what Lord Vaughn said since he was entirely focused on Evelina. Evelina gazed up one final time at the fleeing Cedric, her eyes filled with regret. Cedric turned around and proceeded to the exit. He wasn't going to remain here any longer than necessary. They welcomed the newlyweds and offered their congratulations; it was time for them to go.

"Cedric," Hannah whispered, dragging him to the side as Percival tried his charms on the visitor, who looked at them warily. Cedric saw the situation and relocated them to a more private location on the estate.

"I'm going back," Cedric stated.

"I am not going to babysit one more grown man tonight," Hannah replied, irritated. "So, we go back, we do what we came here to do and then leave."

"Hannah, I can't remain here. You don't realize how difficult it is for me to watch her," Cedric replied, his voice shaking.

"I understand, Cedric," Hannah said quietly. "I was at your apartment. I was serving Lady Caro when she was set to marry Percival. But we're here to tell Evelina the truth, and you'll do it for your own good. I do not want you to have regrets for the rest of your life.

"Hannah, even if I attempted to tell her the truth, there is no way I can get her alone," Cedric remarked irritably "She is surrounded by people all around. Now, unless you want me to proclaim it to the whole crowd in there, I don't see any way to speak to her."

"Not a bad idea," Percival said, earning him incredulous glances from Hannah and Cedric. "Or not." He added.

"I can't believe you're supposed to be the smartest of the four," Hannah replied, angry, disregarding her husband's protests. "Any idiot would know it is impossible to talk to Lady Winchester right now but after all the guest goes home and everyone retires to their chambers, you will have the chance to speak to her," she stated. "Now, how would you know how to reach her chamber if you do not know what Winchester estate looked like from the inside."

Cedric realized she was totally correct. He has to scout the area for potential openings and ensure that he could enter the estate when the party had ended. He has to figure out which was Evelina's room and how to get there, plus he'll need a disguise. Today was the greatest moment to enter the estate since there must be a lot of service personnel there only for the party. They would continue to labour at the estate after everyone had departed. It was an excellent opportunity.

"You are a genius, wife," Percival said, his eyes full of love and admiration.

"Thank you, husband," she said smiling.

"Now, should we return? We have an entire estate to spy on," Percival said for the first time.

"Percival," Cedric said hesitantly, "Are you okay with this?"

"No," Percival said. "I wish you hadn't let her leave the instant you realized you loved her. You missed so many opportunities. I hope you do not make the same mistake again."

"I won't," Cedric said.

Everyone made their way back into the ballroom. Their primary purpose was to discover as many entrances to the estate as possible in order to assess which one was the finest and to locate Evelina's chamber without arousing suspicion. It was more difficult than Cedric expected. The guest entertaining room was fully separate from the family and military members' dwelling quarters. With his regal clothes, Cedric was unable to stroll to the side of his living quarters. Hannah and Percival were also not having much success. Everyone in the crowd wanted to chat with

Percival and his wife, who were seldom seen at the event. They were attempting to conceal all of the hurtful things they said during their wedding by seeming friendly.

Time went swiftly; even though the party was still going on, the Whitworth had overstayed their welcome with the Winchester, thanks in large part to Lord Cedric. They were back in the carriage heading to the Whitworth mansion, each deep in contemplation about how to enter the Winchester estate.

"Do you have anything, Cedric?" Hannah broke the stillness by saying, "We sadly couldn't find anything."

"I know where the family's living quarters are. I need to make sure I enter the correct one," Cedric remarked worriedly. If he makes even the tiniest error, the situation might quickly spiral out of control.

Cedric was dissatisfied with his lack of a concrete strategy. He was usually the methodical one, preparing everything down to the last detail, but this time he doesn't have time for that. He had to trust Evelina's approach, donning a disguise and barging in, hoping for the best. He hired Hackney and dressed in boring, worn-out clothing that was difficult to obtain since his butler refused to share the servants' clothes with him. He generously compensated the hackney driver and asked him to wait as long as he wanted. He waited in the cold and darkness in front of the Winchester estate for what seemed like hours, until the last guests had departed and the service personnel began to work. He knew the estate would not be sleeping tonight, with the wedding just a day away. They need to prepare at night.

Cedric crept inside the estate under the guise of bringing his intoxicated Lord and made his way directly to the stables. He eventually located the person he was seeking: the carriage driver who had stayed outside his mansion all night waiting for his girlfriend. He'd beg if he had to, but he'll make sure this individual helps him locate Evelina. When that man observed Cedric, he instantly recognized him.

"Milord," he said, alerting everyone working there.

In the Arms of a Rake Series

27

Chapter Twenty-seven

Cedric was fast on his feet.
"Where?" Cedric swiftly turned around, scared. "I'm sorry, my friend. I came to see you without informing you, but don't frighten me like this; I nearly wet my pants." Half of the people ignored the two guys and went about their business. Cedric wanted to ensure that they were alone and out of sight of everyone.
"You know I need some money, my friend," Cedric said openly.
"Everything okay there lad?" Someone yelled in the dimly lighted stable.
"This is a buddy from the village. I'll take care of him," he said whomever had called out to him. He moved ahead and pushed Cedric to the opposite side.

"My Lord, you are horrible at acting," he replied, shocking Cedric. He never expected anybody other than Evelina to talk to him so openly.

"What do you want?" He asked.

"I need to meet Lady Evelina."

"Why?"

"That." Cedric wanted to argue it wasn't his business, but if he needed a favor from this man, he'd have to pacify him.

"I have to ask for her Ladyship's forgiveness," Cedric stated truly. The other man gazed at Cedric for some time, trying to figure out whether he was lying.

"I'm only doing this because Lady Evelina has been unhappy since her return from the manor. She walked like a ghost the day I brought her back. I knew it was something you did that made her like that, and I'm simply here to assist you so her Ladyship may be happy again," he replied, narrowing his gaze. When Cedric nodded, he signaled him to follow him. They passed past what seemed to be the servant quarters. It was beyond midnight, and everyone was weary. Some onlookers looked suspiciously at Cedric's menacing stature, but the man guiding him handled everything properly.

"You wait here, if anyone asks tell them you are Tristan's friend," the man added. Cedric stood beside the entrance where Tristan entered. He slapped himself on the back for not yelling at Tristan to hurry up, and what was he doing inside?

In the Arms of a Rake Series

"Cecilia," Tristan said faintly outside, and Cedric's ears pricked up. He opened the door slightly further to hear the talk.

"Please tell me, her Ladyship has retired to her chamber and her despicable fiancé has left," Tristan begged.

"Tristan, her Ladyship, is being married the day after. How can you still be infatuated with her when you know it will end in heartbreak?"

"I'm not obsessed with her Ladyship. I admire her," Tristan remarked, arguing.

"Same thing, different words," the woman continued, paying no attention to Tristan.

"No, it is not. Her ladyship taught me the phrases, and they signify various things," Tristan continued to insist.

"Like you know all the words and their meanings in the language," the lady responded, frustrated.

"At least I know more than you," Tristan said triumphantly.

Cedric restrained himself from meddling. Seriously, do they have the time for this?

"Get out, you arrogant bastard. And find someone else to bother to see whether her Ladyship is okay the next time. For today, her Ladyship has already gone to her room," Cecilia said, forcing Tristan out of her quarters as he attempted to thank her.

"Was that necessary?" Cedric asked Tristan, angry.

"We had to know if her Ladyship is in her chambers or somewhere else in the manor to find her," Tristan replied matter-of-factly.

Cedric disregarded the punch and concentrated on meeting Evelina. They passed through the service doors, and Tristan stood in front of one of them. Cedric realized it was Evelina on the other end. His heart began beating faster.

"My Lord," Tristan stopped his anxieties, "I will guard outside and say her Ladyship called me but I forgot to ask her the details. I'll knock on the door, and that's your signal to hide."

"You're smarter than you look. Where did you learn all of this?" Cedric expressed amazement at the intellect of an ordinary carriage driver.

"Lady Evelina, of course," Tristan said proudly. "She has been sneaking about since she was a toddler, and she had no qualms about playing with military personnel's children. Being just a year older than her Ladyship, I was her company for most of her misbehaviour."

Cedric couldn't believe Tristan's casually said statements. It seemed inconceivable that the Lord and Lady of Winchester would allow their only daughter to play with the servants' children.

"My Lord, we won't have much time," Tristan remarked, motioning him to enter through the entrance. Cedric opened the door gently, looking to see whether anybody other than Evelina was there. He heard Tristan remark, "You better growl at her feet," as he slid inside. Cedric caught his breath as he stood rigidly in place, his back against the service door. His eyes darted around, looking for anybody else who shouldn't be there. Cedric could only hear the crackling of fire in the fireplace and the ruffle of linens from the bed.

He let out a sigh of relief.

He approached gently towards the bed, where he could see Evelina's body hidden behind layers of blankets. He mustered his nerve to speak something as Evelina leaped from the bed to the other side, grabbing the glass from the side table and pointing it at him.

"Evelina," he screamed, praying the glass had not slipped out of her grasp. "Cedric?" She asked: "Is that you?" Cedric noticed that, although brighter than the service corridor, the room was still too dark for them to see each other well. He couldn't believe the first thing he did was startle Evelina by invading her room like a criminal.

"Yes, it is me," Cedric responded, still scared of the weapon in her grip. "If we move closer to the fire, you will be able to see me better." Evelina stepped first, and Cedric proceeded toward the fire, his gaze unable to meet hers. Evelina leaped on Cedric, enveloping him in a crushing embrace, and he almost toppled backwards. Cedric, astonished, took a minute to embrace her back. It felt great to be in her embrace. He could feel her slim frame becoming thinner, and he felt a stab of remorse rise in his gut. Her scent remained the same, and he breathed deeply, soothing his agitated mind.

Cedric felt like all of his vitality had been taken away. In a million years, he never imagined this conclusion. His eyes were wet as he remembered the day he spent worrying over her, and he clutched her even closer. She replied by tightening her grip. Evelina soon fought against him, and Cedric, too scared to let her go, refused to budge.

"I can't breathe," Evelina muttered, causing Cedric to release his grip. She was still in his arms, taking in the air her lungs sorely required. Cedric chastised himself for not understanding how to properly hold a woman. He'd never felt the want to hug someone so near. But with Evelina, he wanted them to blend into one other so they couldn't tell where she stopped and he started. Evelina held him tightly after she had taken in enough breath. Even though Cedric wanted to remain like this forever, he realized he had a time restriction here.

"Evelina," he said, tenderly rubbing his fingers on the back of her head. "I need to tell you something."

"What is it, my Lord?" She said burying her nose in his shoulder.

"About the ledger," he explained carefully.

"You are going to tell me you weren't a part of it," She spoke in an optimistic tone. He knew that was what she wanted to hear. But Cedric was here to reveal the truth without considering the ramifications.

"I was," he said, hardening his heart. But it stung more than he expected when she left his arms and took a step back, her anguish palpable in her eyes.

*In the Arms of a Rake Series*

28

Chapter Twenty-eight

Cedric knew he had opened the gates of hell when he revealed his involvement in the Ledger's coverage of her Library catastrophe. But he was here to tell her the whole truth, and he was willing to suffer whatever punishment she gave him.

"I can explain everything," Cedric said seriously.

"Does it matter?" Evelina said tersely.

"It does, it matters, please listen to me," He said, "I want to be straight with you. I don't want to be a deceptive, lying politician to you. I just want to be myself in front of you." Evelina stared at Cedric.

"Let's have a seat," Evelina murmured monotonously. "Let us tell each other all the truths and see if we can forgive each other."

"Evelina," Cedric exclaimed in anguish. It was as if their roles were inverted. She was suddenly stone cold, and Cedric could scarcely restrain his feelings.

"You should start first because you made such an effort to come here," Evelina remarked harshly.

"Evelina," Cedric said once again, hoping she'd return to herself and stop acting so coldly toward him. When Evelina refused to bend, Cedric had no option but to reveal the truth. He didn't have much time and couldn't go without doing what he came here to do. He needed to confess his truth, not to console her, but to liberate himself from guilt.

"It is true that I was behind your library escapade published in the ledger," Cedric remarked, his gaze fixed on his feet, unable to look at her. "It is true, but not in the way everyone thinks," he said, looking at her. She was trying hard not to cry. Cedric reacted without thinking and embraced her once again. Evelina didn't make an attempt to walk away, nor did she hug him back. It hurt Cedric's heart; he wished he could erase the past, but then he would have never met her or felt love.

He was living a joyful, carefree life until she came into his life like a cyclone, and he wouldn't change a thing. Without all that transpired, he would never have realized how much of his soul belonged to her.

"It is silly, so stupid of me to get drunk that night," Cedric said while still holding her. "I was irritated that Percival did not consider my profession and that I had to fake in front of the world. The world believed all of us Whitworths stood united for Percival, but my family felt I was against them and the world, so I ended myself alone. Nobody stopped to consider how much I had to give up. It is not fair."

Cedric paused breathing in order to avoid entirely breaking down in front of her. Nobody realized how much his surroundings affected him. That his aspirations and the profession he had fought for would be ripped away in an instant by the acts of others around him.

"I did not allow selfish ideas to take over. Nobody owed me their life. But that night, everything came crashing down on me, and I, like any other foolish man, buried myself in wine," he added, tears streaming down his cheeks.

"I was so drunk that when a party member came to me about how he may use your name against your father by appearing innocent news in the ledger, I offered my approval without thinking anything about it." Evelina pulled away from him as he confessed.

"Do you mean to tell me you were intoxicated while you decided to add more stain to my reputation?" Evelina asked fiercely. Cedric remained mute, nodding in response to her inquiry, and kept his lips shut for fear of saying anything wrong.

"You were intoxicated while consenting to what seemed like a harmless thing for you," Evelina queried defeatedly

"What should I do now? Excuse yourself because you were intoxicated or it was harmless to you? Do you realize how much I endured before that? It was the last straw for me, too."

"My actions cannot be forgiven because I was intoxicated. Neither do I have the right to pass judgment on what may be harmless or harmful to you," Cedric said. He recognized the consequences of his actions, but it was too late.

"If I could I wish I would go back and change so many things if that meant you would not suffer," Cedric stated with tears in his eyes. "But there is this selfish part of me that does not want to change anything, afraid it might change everything and I would never get to stand in front of you here."

"I don't know what to do, Cedric," Evelina muttered in despair. "But I understand. I am scared that if I alter anything in the past, I will cease to exist for you. And it hurts me more than anything. There's this sense that I don't comprehend the accompanying guilt, which makes it much more difficult to interpret." Cedric lacked the courage to identify that sensation. What if he says something and it's not true? Cedric refrained from taking a risk at this moment.

"Why have you come here? What did you anticipate from this meeting? What do you want from me?" Evelina inquired.

"I wanted to liberate myself," Cedric replied quietly, "And find some peace after telling you the truth. I wanted to let go of this enormous load on my chest."

"Is that all?" Evelina inquired, her expression bland.

"Yes," Cedric said gently.

"You do not want my forgiveness," she inquired quietly, her fury gone.

"I do not deserve it."

"And what about me? I fooled you, too."

"We both did terrible things to one another, but it was all due to my foolish mistake." Cedric interrupted her, "It was I who started all this. You do not need to ask me for forgiveness, but if you feel remorseful, I have one request."

"What is it?" Evelina inquired apprehensively.

"Can we put the past behind ourselves?" He inquired optimistically. Everything was really complex. It wasn't simple to go over everything they'd done in the past, nor was it easy to blindly forgive everyone, but they needed to find a way to go on.

"What about the future? What if I did something that will affect your future?" she questioned quietly.

"What do you mean?" Cedric inquired, not understanding her.

"I did something to save myself," she murmured, looking away from him.

"If it is to save yourself, I do not mind at all," Cedric murmured, reaching out to her.

"Do not be hasty, my Lord," Evelina stated sternly. "You discovered my message at the Whitworth manor. It never reached my parents. They assumed I was carrying your child. I couldn't bear for them to look at me with those eyes," Evelina said, her voice wavering.

Cedric hugged her. His arms enveloped her waist, and her back rested on his chest, giving her comfort.

"I informed them about the inheritance law. The Conservative Party is ready. They want to smash it on its debut appearance." Evelina muttered, "You will not be able to win, Cedric." She pulled herself away from his arms and confronted him. Her face was devoid of expression.

"I did it so you would experience at least part of the agony I feel. I did it to cause you to suffer. Now tell me, would you forgive me?"

Cedric stood frozen. How could she do that after everything? She understood how crucial this was for him. The person he loves has deceived him. The feelings were a combination of hatred and love, fury and despair. His mind couldn't think clearly, but he knew he still loved her. However, being in love does not guarantee happiness. Loving her does not allow him to pretend she never purposefully crushed his heart. Love does not ensure happily ever after.

Despite the sorrow, he wanted to spend his life with her. He was willing to endure in order to be with her forever.

"You should leave now," Evelina's words echoed in the calm room. His agony and suffering would be meaningless if she too suffered. He couldn't bear the anguish of watching her suffer. Cedric kissed her temple softly and turned to go.

In the Arms of a Rake Series

29

Chapter Twenty-nine

Today was Evelina's wedding. Cedric was at his own estate. He was surrounded by sorrow as his family prepared to attend the wedding of the lady he loved and abandoned. Despite recognizing Cedric's stance against Lord Winchester, his family believed it would be completely wrong for them not to attend the wedding, and they asked Cedric to accompany them for the sake of his political image.

But Cedric didn't want to consider that the lady he loved might marry another man. He intended to dwell in obscurity for as long as he could. He wanted to believe that they would still meet at another ball and try to get each other's attention. He fantasized about once again shielding Evelina from her father as she sneaked into his office.

He wanted to dream a little longer. She would rush into his estate, her red hair untamed and freckles visible. He would then converse with her, going from one subject to the next and being caught in another fantastical journey that came to mind. He intended to take her to his duchy in Silvershire. They might attempt to find all of the old palace's hidden corridors and rooms, as well as wander around the perimeter of the flower fields to hear the sound of water dripping someplace deep under the mountain.

He had a strong desire to live with her. He could only dream now, for the truth was becoming clear as Evelina went down the aisle. He pondered how she would seem in her white bridal gown. Her wedding gown hugged her slim waist, and her hair was precisely styled atop her head, with a wayward strand escaping and running through the veil. Simply the angel that would approach him. But why was she approaching him with her skirt bunched up in her hand?

Cedric glanced around anxiously and realized he was seated in his estate's garden. He glanced back and saw her barging at him, her lips mumbling. He could tell she was swearing based on her look. Cedric sat erect in his seat. Was he hallucinating?

He tried phoning the folks in his home, but following his pathetic appeal to leave him alone, they all scampered off to their jobs. There was no one to help him get out of this. It was a nightmare for Cedric. He didn't want to wake up without Evelina in his life. He closed his eyes firmly, wishing to awaken from this dreadful dream. Evelina couldn't have been here. It was her wedding day, for goodness sake. He prayed to relieve his suffering, but it did not help. But suddenly a notion flashed over his mind. Could it be real? Evelina always did things that no one else would consider doing. He opened his eyes slightly, and Evelina stood before him, gasping for air.

"Will," she said enthusiastically as their eyes met.

"Evelina," Cedric said softly, "What brings you here?" He still felt like he was dreaming.

"I thought a walk and some fresh air would do me good," Evelina said, still regaining her breath. "It is quite stuffy in this darn dress."

"That is a wedding dress," Cedric replied, still unsure whether it was real or a dream.

"Ah, yeah," Evelina laughed, "The wedding. It slipped my mind."

"It is your bloody wedding," Cedric said emphatically.

"Yes, I remember," Evelina answered, bored. "I also remember what marriage stands for me."

"And what is that?" Cedric inquired, puzzled.

"For me, marriage stands for love and loyalty," Evelina remarked, a little grin on her lips. "I could never love that prick of a man who is my fiancé, but I figured I could be loyal to him."

"Then why are you here?" Cedric questioned, plunging back into reality.

"Because marriage is holy for me and I have sinned," Evelina whispered with tears in her eyes. "I can't marry anyone else for, pardon my language, for I have already been with you as husband and wife are supposed to be on their wedding night."

Cedric staggered in shock. She told him she couldn't marry anybody else since he had slept with her. The notion made him thrilled, but also uneasy since he had wrecked her. He damaged the angel and was unworthy of her.

"I apologize, Evelina," Cedric whispered remorsefully, to the point of tears. He couldn't do more than apologize. "I should've been a better man. I should not have given in to my instincts. And it's worse since we were under the effect of drinks," he said.

"Now, there is no need to lie; you were under the effect of alcohol, while I was perfectly sober. I seduced and compromised you, therefore I'm asking Cedric Whitworth to elope with me and marry me; I promise to keep you happy forever," she stated gallantly.

Cedric gazed at Evelina, bewildered.

"This is not how it works, Evelina," he responded, perplexed.

"Why not!" She hollered, "If a lady can have control of her fortune and as in your vision has the right to get the same education as the gentleman, god forbid the freedom to vote and have a profession like men, then why can't a lady ask a man she loves for his hand in marriage." Cedric's eyes widen in horror. The man she adores! Did he hear her correctly?

"The man you love," he said, perplexed.

"Now, don't break my heart, Cedric," she urged, her face tearing up. The vulnerable side of her emerged.

In the Arms of a Rake Series

"You love me?" He questioned her, still shocked.

"And here I thought you were one of the smartest politicians in the kingdom," she replied hesitantly. She was attempting to be strong in the face of rejection.

"Evelina," he whispered, his eyes welling with tears.

"Yes, I love you," she said, her cheeks heating up. "Now, we will need to leave before my father realizes I am missing from my own wedding."

"Evelina," he whispered, halting her.

Her heart broke. He seldom addressed her by name, which signaled he was likely to reject her. He would tell her he did not want her. She never pondered his decisions, despite the fact that she knew there was a person behind this frigid man.

"How can you be so nonchalant about this?" He inquired incredulously.

"I'm not. I am completely serious," she said.

"Are you certain you want to marry me?"

"Yes."

"Ledger will again run a mile with your name on it,"

"I know."

"Ghastlier, rumours than before."

"Yes, I can see them already thinking about it."

"Once we are married there won't be any way out."

"Cedric!"

"I won't let you."

"What?"

"I won't let you leave ever, no matter how much we break each other's heart, how much we hurt each other, I will forever love you," he said. Evelina made a daring move, capturing his lips in hers. Cedric tightened his grip on her and intensified their kiss. They eventually had to part ways since someone coughed too loudly for humans.

"My Lady, my Lord," the butler replied, looking away from them. "The carriage is prepared if you are. It's better to make haste."

"What for?" Cedric inquired.

"The Lady said she's eloping with you and needs a carriage that won't be recognized as Winchester's or Whitworth's," His butler casually said. Cedric returned Evelina's stare with amusement. She was prepared, and the prospect of eloping with her excited him. He was a stickler for regulations, but this time he felt better about violating them. It was as if she were saying an adventure.

"It's now or never," she whispered, reading his thoughts. Indeed! It was a lifetime of adventure with her, and Cedric was excited to begin.

"Pray that your father or fiancé do not find us before we reach Gretna Green," Cedric said enthusiastically.

"They will not. Your butler arranged the carriage for us, and I brought my own driver," Evelina said. They made their way to the carriage. The driver who had previously transported her was already waiting for them.

"Are we really doing this?" Cedric questioned as they sat inside and the carriage started to move.

"No, no, wait," Evelina said, "I forgot to do this." Cedric's heart halted for a second as he feared she might go. She clasped his hands in hers and let out a loud sigh.

"Cedric Whitworth, will you fancy eloping with me?"

30

Chapter Thirty

Cedric was transfixed at the doorway, thinking about what he would say to his family on the other side. Evelina thought it amusing. He should be soothing her as they go to see his family after they eloped and married at Gretna Green. Cedric took a big breath, and Evelina giggled because he was worried about nothing. Evelina did not bother if his family refused to accept her. She knows how to hold her ground. She would put up with Cedric's folks as long as he was around. She was never going to beg him to leave anybody, but she was certainly not going to stand there and accept any rudeness.

She had no fear of what was ahead. It seemed like another adventure for her. She was so happy that she wanted to rush in and inform everyone that she had eloped and married their son, Cedric Whitworth. She was quite thrilled. It wasn't exactly as she had envisioned her wedding, but she did marry her Prince charming, whom she adores and who adores her in return.

She didn't mind the hurried wedding. Eloping was not something she anticipated. She wanted to be married in a church, with her father escorting her down the aisle. Cedric is waiting at the other end. But this was far more enjoyable than her desire. She knew she'd have to ask her parents for forgiveness and the extravagant wedding she'd always dreamed of.

The idea of her parents helped her understand why Cedric was feeling the way he did. But instead of thinking about all the things she should say and do, the reality would remain the same. She'd rather get it over with than worry about it later. Finally, Cedric seemed to have made up his mind as he instructed the footmen to open the door. The sight inside was not what was anticipated. Everyone was busy decorating the parlour, and orders were flying about everywhere. It seemed like the preparation was being done quickly.

"Cedric," Evelina murmured, pulling on his shirt sleeve. "Is there any celebration planned?"

"No, nothing," Cedric said, stunned.

Everyone was so preoccupied with their job that no one spotted the pair standing and observing the pandemonium for a long time. Cedric considered slipping past the throng to the bedroom and resting before breaking the news to the family. The journey to Gretna Green and back had taken its toll on their bodies, but they had just hidden it behind the excitement. But now they could feel the fatigue setting in. Cedric whispered his idea to Evelina, and she realized he was attempting to avoid notifying his family.

She grinned knowingly and agreed to his proposal. She, too, needed to collect her strength if she was to confront the fury of the Whitworths. But before they could go two steps farther, someone whispered, bringing everyone to a stop and turning all eyes on them. They're here! They're here! Cedric could hear everyone whispering and praying it wasn't them they were looking for. There was no way he would be prepared so well, but if his mother knew he would be returning with a wife, she would go out of her way to prepare.

Everyone filed out of the parlour in a slow and efficient manner. His mother was the first to arrive, followed by Hannah. She hurriedly approached them when she saw them standing at the entrance. His mother's expression made it apparent she understood. He gave Hannah a sour look when she ratted him out.

"Cedric, my dear darling," his mother murmured cheerfully, attempting to embrace his towering figure. Cedric bowed down to allow his mother to kiss him on the cheek, then kissed her on the forehead. His mother's enthusiasm warmed his heart. He has always had the strongest connection to his mother. She was the source of his motivation and confidence. He was no longer terrified.

"Mother," he began firmly. "I'd like to introduce you to my wife, Lady Evelina Winchester." Mother Whitworth squinted her eyes at the pair and said, "Wife?" Cedric gasped at his mother's inquiry.

"I want pardon for marrying without your permission. But I hope you will accept us," he said.

"What if I don't?" His mother inquired, folding her hands. Cedric was taken aback for a minute; he had not anticipated his mother to respond this way. She was delighted to receive Hannah and Percival, and her reservations about embracing Evelina made little sense to him.

"My Lady," Evelina addressed his mother directly, "I am delighted to meet you. I realize how stunned you are by your son's news but I'd want to clarify that I am the one who abducted your son and eloped with him. I asked him to marry me at Gretna Green. So, whatever penalty you choose, I will willingly take it." Mother Whitworth was in awe of Evelina. She gave Hannah an astonished expression. She arched an eyebrow at Cedric since he hadn't responded yet.

"I-I," Cedric stuttered. "I love her." He knew his mother needed to hear this. Lady Whitworth laughed. She could have overextended her enjoyment. Evelina grasped Cedric's finger softly. She may have miscalculated the consequences of his family's rejection. But his mother smiled brightly and kissed Evelina's forehead.

"Pardon me for my actions. I wondered whether my son married you for the right reasons. I don't want any woman in my house to be with a man who doesn't love her," Lady Whitworth explained to Evelina.

"The moment you entered my home as my son's bride, there was no place for any other worthless ideas. Welcome to our family, dear."

Evelina's eyes wet, and she held Lady Whitworth warmly without hesitation. She prayed her own mother would welcome her in the same manner, but she knew the reality would be quite different.

When a commotion broke out in the parlour, she didn't have time to think about it.

"They are really here," someone remarked. Evelina instantly recognized the bright green eyes. It was Lord Octavian, Whitworth's third son.

"Why are you standing there like a fool?" He remarked to Cedric: "Introduce us to your bride." Cedric wrapped his arms around Evelina's waist, directing her towards everyone. He presented his father, brothers, Hannah, and twins one at a time.

"Where is Percival?" Cedric inquired as to when everyone had settled down for tea and nibbles.

"He is hiding from you," Hannah answered his queries. "He thinks you will berate him for telling Mother about you and Evelina."

"It was him," Cedric remarked, puzzled.

"Yes. You assumed that was me, didn't you? Hannah gave him the same critical look he had given her a few minutes before.

"You should go talk to him," Dom said.

"No, let him suffer a little more," Cedric said.

Evelina could not believe it. It seemed like her wishful thinking. She never anticipated things to be so simple, and yet she was already a member of the family. Everyone was chatting about the wedding preparations as if she hadn't just eloped with Cedric and wedded in Gretna Green.

"We will need to hastily prepare for the wedding, I think we will be adequately prepared in a month from now," she stated. "There is so much to do."

"Mother," Cedric said, "Let's set a date for the end of this week."

"That is not enough time," his mother said.

"I agree, I do want a lavish wedding if I can get one," Evelina said with excitement.

Cedric sighed. It seemed that his whole family would oppose him, but he had more pressing concerns. He didn't want to talk too soon and destroy the moment, but he had to explain why he wanted the wedding to happen as soon as possible.

"I am worried about Lord Winchester," Cedric replied with great caution. "I do not want to give him time to find anything that will take Evelina away from me." Everyone stared at Cedric with renewed awe. They had no idea Cedric could care so deeply for someone. He exuded satisfaction every time he looked at Evelina. The air was full of content.

"No one can take her away from you," Percival remarked from the doorway. "You married in the church in front of God and witnesses. To establish this, your marriage certificate must include the signatures of two witnesses."

"Well, about that!" Cedric said.

31

Chapter Thirty-one

"What do you mean by that? About what?" Hannah was the one who asked Cedric. "Do not tell me you eloped with Evelina and didn't marry her," she said angrily.

"Will," Evelina murmured with wide eyes, "We made our vows. We had witnesses. We're married." She could not believe Cedric was going to reveal their secret. She hoped Cedric understood what she was trying to say to him, which was to keep his mouth shut.

"Evelina," Cedric continued casually, "I'm just scared about your father finding out. If we reveal the truth here, we will be safe from undesirable difficulties. Cedric stared at Evelina, and they spoke to each other via their eyes.

"The suspense is killing me," Octavian said, prompting the pair to break out of their eye match. His father whacked him on the head for doing so.

"Don't worry; we'll be there for you no matter what," Percival added, beaming broadly at Evelina and patting Cedric on the back.

"Unless you haven't married yet," Hannah said, her gaze narrowing.

"So..," Octavian asked anxiously. Everyone waited with bated breath to hear what Cedric would say.

"One of the witnesses was underage," Cedric said cautiously. The feelings on everyone's faces ranged from astonishment to anxiety.

"How much underage?" His father inquired.

"Well," Cedric paused. "He was seven years old and could write his name." Nobody knows why Octavian broke out laughing at such a serious situation. The twins copied him, and the whole room burst into laughter and grins.

"If someone finds out it will make your marriage invalid," His father yelled something out, for which he was whacked in the head by his mother. Even if it was said in jest, it was true. They cannot afford to lose any time. The lavish wedding will take longer to arrange. Evelina valued her relationship with Cedric above the grandiose wedding.

"How about we have a wedding in three days?" Looking at her audience, Evelina said, "It doesn't have to be as lavish a wedding as we would want. It might be a casual gathering of family and friends or a solemn ceremony in church. And after everything has calmed down, a magnificent reception."

"Why darling?" Lady Whitworth expressed concern, "Everyone should have a magnificent wedding. And I'm certain that I can plan an elaborate event in a matter of days."

"I believe in you, dear Lady," Evelina murmured regretfully, beaming at Lady Whitworth. "But the lavish event will be without my parents. Once they accept us, I swear we will arrange a lavish reception for months and host a party like London has never seen before."

Everyone remained quiet. She was correct. Everyone knew her parents would not take it so casually.

"Today is your special day. We will do everything as you desire," Mother Whitworth murmured, clutching Evelina's hand to reassure the young bride.

"And it is not my Lady to you anymore, it is mother and father," she went on to say. Father Whitworth nodded from behind.

"And can we call you Evelina or Evy, Evelina is too long to call, if you are alright with it?" Octavian asked openly.

Before Evelina could respond, Cedric interfered.

"No, you cannot call her Evelina," he told her. "Only I can call her Evelina."

"Oh my goodness," Tavi said, "Cedric is human again." Everyone laughed, and Cedric appeared moderately offended.

"Lady Evelina, please do not mind, Tavi," Dom responded politely. "We do not mind calling you by your proper title."

Evelina questioned how these two could be brothers.

Many people mistake them for twins, despite the fact that they are quite different in many aspects. Dom was attempting to undo what Tavi had done since he believed he should not have been so brazen with her. But Evelina wanted to be a member of this family. She wanted everyone to feel at ease with her and to identify as a Whitworth.

"May I call you Dom?" Evelina questioned, smiling.

"Absolutely," Dom said, drawing a laugh from Percival. Dom's eagerness to see Evelina was not lost on anybody in the parlour.

"Then you may call me Evy," she said, adding, "All my family calls me Evy."

"How about Evy? I'd like to annoy Cedric," Tavi said, hoping.

"I approve," Evy said, drawing critical eyes from Cedric.

"Evy it is!" Tavi suggested lifting an imaginary glass to toast.

Everyone spoke for a bit before moving on to lunch. Evelina and Cedric did not get much sleep, and their mother directed them to separate bedrooms after lunch.

"Is it because of our wedding witness?" Evelina questioned Cedric quietly as she walked down the aisle.

"No, she did it to us too," Hannah replied from the front, where she had been ordered by their mother together with Percival to ensure that her directions were carried out and that the newlyweds remained apart.

"Why?" Evelina inquired.

"I guess she wants us to experience how it would be if we had a wedding like others," Hannah stated warmly.

"The anticipation, the desire and waiting, the ticking of the clock. She wants us to go through everything so that everything seems more precious and genuine. More real!"

Evelina felt like she was living a dream when she married the man she loved. However, she did not wish to spend her wedding night in separate bedrooms.

"I think she's punishing you," Tavi murmured from behind them. Dom and Tavi joined the two couples for fun, and everyone has since attempted to ignore the cheeky trio in the back.

"Why would she punish them, Tavi?" Dom inquired significantly.

"Oh you know how Mother is about the weddings," he remarked.

"Tavi," Cedric remarked without turning back, "Even if she's punishing us, it'll be over in a few days. But remember, you're next on her list."

"You mean Dom is next on her list," he said, "I think everyone knows it would take a miracle for me to get married."

"You never know, that miracle might just be around the corner," Evelina murmured, looking up at Cedric.

She discovered her miracle, and as she looked about, her concern about Whitworths rejecting her faded.

"I would love to see that," Dom replied, eliciting a playful jab from Tavi. The conversation continued until they had to split. Hannah led Evelina to her designated bedroom, while the males followed Cedric to his. Evelina was successful in slipping away and meeting Cedric in his bedchamber, knowing the route.

She also discovered that her bedchamber was closer to Hannah's and knew she would have to inform the couple that the man there after the twins' birth was indeed her.

The family reconnected during dinnertime. Evelina had a great time playing with the twins and could not get enough of them. She spoke with Dom and Tavi as if they had reconnected after a long absence. She felt she had always belonged here. It had only been a few hours when she realized she wanted to be here with not just Cedric, but the whole Whitworth family. She was so joyful and free. After supper, everyone sat in the parlour and enjoyed the company of their loved ones.

Evelina saw that the environment surrounding her had become hushed, and an uneasy sensation had settled over her. She glanced away from the twins to see Cedric standing next to Percival, both of them staring at the evening newspaper.

"What is it?" She inquired, capturing everyone's attention. "Will," she said, her voice trembling.

Cedric opened his lips to say something but was unable to find the correct words. He sat alongside her, kissing her temple and resting his hands on her waist for support.

"Evelina, I am here with you," Cedric whispered, massaging her back, "For every step and whatever you decide. We are all with you. I love you," he muttered just to her.

"Will, you're scaring me," Evelina replied, somewhat worried. He handed her the evening newspaper hesitantly.

Lord Winchester, the Conservative Party leader, has resigned. His daughter had eloped.

Former Prime Minister and leader of the Conservative Party has resigned from his leadership position and announced his retirement from parliament, putting his almost three-decade political career to an end. This statement comes after his only daughter vanished from her wedding and eloped with her boyfriend.

In the Arms of a Rake Series

32

Chapter Thirty-two

Evelina had never felt so furious and heartbroken before. She couldn't believe how quickly her forgetfulness would pass. She knew she had to confront her parents, but she was trying to muster some strength before facing their displeasure. But first, she needed to do something else.
"Where is the ledger's office?" She inquired about the dead silence chamber. No one spoke, their eyes fixed on her outraged expression. Everyone there knew what it meant when someone said that looks could kill. She was more terrible than Cedric, and no one dared say anything.
"Why?" Hannah inquired quietly, not wanting to frighten her anymore. Evelina didn't respond, her gaze remained fixed on the news piece.

Cedric drew her into his arms and gently rubbed her head, soothing her down. He had an idea why she wanted to go to the ledger's office. She was furious, but deep down she was wounded, and that needed to be addressed first.

"Why do you wanna go to the Ledger's office, Evy?" Hannah inquired again cautiously.

"I want to burn down their office," Evelina screamed, breaking away from Cedric. "Their audacity to publish something like this in the newspaper for everyone to see. Why would they lie and claim my father is retired? He likes what he does and has not retired. If they want to insult me, they may, but why bring my father into it?"

"Evy, why don't we have someone clear the ledger's building first? You don't want anybody injured if we set the workplace on fire, do you?" Hannah uttered something surprising to everyone in the room.

Everyone, including Evy, turned their heads to Hannah, surprised and shocked.

"I can do it, burn down the ledger's office?" Evelina expressed amazement. Her rage subsided.

"If you want to, but the livelihood of many who work in the Ledger will be jeopardized, and we will have to pay for the damages done as well as some legal issues, not to mention that we would be criminals," Hannah replied seriously, wondering what else may happen.

"So, we can't do it," Evy pouted.

"Of course, we can, we will need to think this through first," she said.

"What else can I do?" Evelina expressed frustration, "What they've done is wrong. And they won't even be penalized for it?"

"Well, you can speak with your parents." Hannah urged that he ask Ledger to publicly apologize. Evelina remained quiet, anticipating meeting her parents. She wasn't prepared yet. She did not want to be apart from Cedric. She was afraid her parents would take Cedric from her.

"We can go together if you want," Cedric proposed.

"You will come with me?" Evy expressed amazement.

"Yes," he said, "Even though one witness was underage, I did vow in front of that innocent soul that I would always be there with you, every step of the way, against all odds." Evelina grinned, despite her fury. She adored the perfect man.

"I'll never be prepared to face my parents. Which child wants to stir their parent's anger and get scolded?" Evelina moaned.

"My third seemed to do just that all the time," Lady Whitworth replied, turning to face Tavi. Everyone laughed, but Tavi merely pouted.

"Darling," Father Whitworth continued, "We'll all be here when you return. We are now part of your family as well."

With everyone's consoling comments, Evelina prepared to meet her parents. She had no idea what to say to them; would they refuse to meet her? Would they be furious? She preferred it if they were angry. Her mind was racing, going from one terrible notion to another. The only reason she wasn't paDoming was because Cedric was there to soothe her.

They sat in the carriage, her hands in his, and he made sure she knew he was there with his reassuring words and charming actions. They landed at Winchester Manor. The frightening structure was as ancient as the royal residence itself. No one stopped them on the way; everyone let Cedric and Evelina walk through. She seemed to know where her parents would be in this large mansion. She moved ahead, and Cedric followed without question.

Instead of meeting her parents, they ended up in her quarters.

"Evelina," Cedric said, "Why are we here? Shouldn't we meet your parents?"

"Yes, the dinner will be served in a couple of hours," She replied casually as she went through her clothes, "I will change into proper attire and we can meet them at the dinner."

"We shouldn't be here," Cedric remarked, approaching her. Evelina whirled around to face him; her rage evident. "And why not?" She inquired, "This is my chamber."

"Darling," Cedric whispered sweetly to comfort his wife, "The circumstances have changed."

"And it is still my chamber," Evelina said firmly before returning to searching through her clothing. Cedric grabbed her softly from behind, grabbing her hands, and locked them in an embrace. He pressed a delicate kiss across her cheek.

"Why don't we call for your lady-in-waiting and get ready for the dinner," he said. Evelina lay in Cedric's arms for a long time. She didn't want to leave her cocoon of comfort.

The service-woman waiting at her door was not your typical maid who would dress her up. And when she stood panting at the threshold, it seemed as if she had run the whole distance.

"My Lady," she whispered under her breath. She realized her error and straightened her back, curtsying to them.

"My Lady," she replied politely, "At your service. What would you like me to do?" She added nervously, unsure how to talk to aristocratic women.

"Will you help me find an evening gown and then help dress me up?" Evelina inquired, attempting to make the lady in front of her comfortable. The woman's face brightened up, and she nodded vigorously.

"I will be in the waiting area," Cedric remarked, kissing Evelina's temple before departing.

The lady continued struggling to assist Evelina. She realized that wasn't her typical task. When Evelina was ready, she dismissed the maid. She wanted a few minutes to herself. However, the lady was still standing in the hallway.

"Do you need something?" Evelina inquired, drawing the lady out of her thoughts.

"We are very happy you are back, my Lady," she said. Evelina was astonished, but the words put her at ease.

"Thank you," she said gently, her grin bright.

"Can I ask you something, my Lady?" The maid inquired hesitantly.

"Mmmh," Evelina said encouragingly. The maid paused for a long time. She was terrified of something. She was attempting to put together the question in the best way possible. Evelina knew her situation.

"It's fine, you don't have to think so much," Evelina remarked, smiling.

"My Lady," she continued, her voice shaking. "Did Tristan accompany you? Is he okay? Will he be penalized for joining you? Where is he?" Evelina saw her maid softly crumbling in front of her from the inside.

"He is okay. I assume he is being properly cared for at Whitworth Manor." Evelina reassured her, "And I promise he won't be punished for anything. You need not worry." Evelina sent her back after she thanked her warmly. She joined Cedric in the waiting area and headed to the dining room to meet her parents.

"What made you smile so much?" Cedric inquired.

"My coachman is going to get chewed out by his lady after he returns," she chuckled. Evelina's happiness rubbed off on Cedric, and he knew deep down that he would do everything to make her happy even if it meant kneeling down to his opponent, whom she refers to as father. They strolled with a bright grin on their faces and entered the dining hall, where her parents were waiting. Her ex-fiancé, Lord Vaughn, was also there.

33

Chapter Thirty-three

When Cedric confronted Lord Vaughn in the parlour, his blood boiled with wrath. He recalled Evelina's face as she was anguished about what Lord Vaughn had done to her. His jaws stiffened, and his palms tightened into fists. He scowled at Lord Vaughn, forgetting he was there to chastise Evelina's parents.

"What is he doing here?" Evelina was the one who spoke. Her voice was harsh, yet Cedric felt a sense of dread as she grabbed his palm harder. His first focus was her. He took deep breaths to control his fury and focused all of his concentration on his wife. She was his wife. The concept alone made him grin, and his protectiveness took on a new tone.

"What is he doing here?" Evelina requested again, this time glancing at her parents. Nobody answered Evelina's query. Everyone stood there gazing at each other. Lord Winchester, her father, summoned the butler and instructed them to accompany Evelina and Cedric to the dining hall, advising them not to wait for them.

"No," Evelina refused to go, "I want to know why Lord Vaughn is here."

"Are you going to sit still now too?" Lord Vaughn stated furiously while rising, "Your daughter made a fool of me by eloping and now brings a Whitworth as a husband, and you sit there like a damn statue."

"What are you threatening my parents with this time?" Evelina yelled at Lord Vaughn. Offended by her remarks, he lunged at her, angry.

Cedric stood higher in front of Evelina, like a fearsome tiger, which caused Lord Vaughn to halt in his tracks.

"You need to throw him out and your daughter," Vaughn added. "They didn't leave us to show our face anywhere."

"Please," Lord Winchester murmured, straining his teeth, "Don't cause a scene in my house. Everyone standing in this parlour is a visitor; we don't want to offend anybody, so please settle down and do what we say." Evelina walked straight and sat on the sofa.

"I'm not standing," she stated, "And this is also my home." Her antics caused her father to snort, a grin emerging and gone in an instant.

"Evy," her mother urged, "Please proceed to dinner with Lord Silvershire. We will join you soon." Before Evelina could ask any more questions, Cedric placed a hand on her shoulder.

"My Lord, My Lady," Cedric addressed the Winchesters for the first time. "I had numerous speeches prepared on how I would address you for the first time, and in each one, I intended to tell you how much I love Evelina and that I would do anything in this world for her. But the circumstance requires something more from me." He paused, allowing his words to fall on everyone in the parlour.

"I don't intend to upset you in any way, and I'm saying this with good intentions. I married your daughter, and whether you like it or not, I am your son-in-law, and my family is now your family. And we Whitworths would do everything for our families. I want you to know that I am now standing alongside you." Everyone remained silent as they contemplated his comments.

"And what about your standing in parliament against us?" Lady Winchester inquired carefully.

"Family members may have different beliefs and opinions, but it does not mean we cease being a family. We argue with our family members more than we do with others about a variety of issues, but at the end of the day, we want to sit down with them and have a meal," he stated.

"Stop your bullshit," Lord Vaughn said. Cedric fixed Lord Vaughn with a deadly glance.

"Lord Vaughn," he snarled with clenched teeth, "If you ever look at my wife again, I will slit your throat." Lord Vaughn' neck tingled with terror as a result of his remarks. Everyone in the parlour stood staring at Cedric. He gave Evelina a tight-lipped grin and extended his hand.

She gripped his arm and drew calming circles in his palm to calm him down. They strolled to the dining hall, and her parents joined them shortly after sending Lord Vaughn on his way.

The supper was met with an uneasy silence. Nobody dared to utter another word. Once everyone had gone to the parlour, Lord Winchester was the first to speak.

"Lord Silvershire," Her father replied, "Don't think I've welcomed you as family; far from it. And don't give your family's assistance so casually. Winchester's reputation may not be as high as Whitworth's, but we know how to handle ourselves."

"I apologize," Cedric murmured, bowing his head. "I did not mean to offend you."

"I would like to speak with my daughter alone," Lord Winchester remarked, dismissing Cedric. Instead of being insulted, Cedric graciously bowed and exited the parlour, but not before whispering to Evelina that he would wait for her.

He was not upset at all. He recalled it was all for Evelina's sake. And for her, he didn't mind being educated. He realized he had a lot to prove to her parents. She was their only child, so they wanted the best for her. It was not required that what you believe is best for others be also best for them. Sometimes our thinking is a little warped. He realized this when he opposed Percival and Hannah's marriage. He believed in Evelina and his love. He knew she would come back to him; all he had to do was wait for her. He hoped her parents understood even a little bit back in the parlour.

Evelina was seated on the couch, her gaze fixed on the ground. Her parents hadn't spoken since Cedric departed. She wasn't sure if she should be the first to speak.

"Evy," her mom remarked. They addressed her as Evy. Evelina lighted up like a Christmas tree. She knew her biggest dread was not reality. Her parents have not disowned her.

"I am very sorry, mother, and father," Evelina stated genuinely. "I know you are really furious with me. I did not want it to happen this way. I am really sorry." She gazed up at her parents, tears in her eyes. Her father let out a big sigh and nodded his head from side to side.

"Please do not give up on me." Evelina continued thinking and praying.

"Oh, we are so foolish," her father remarked.

"Father," Evelina whispered, her voice cracking. Her father rose and sat down near Evelina. He placed his arms around her in a loving hug.

"Oh, my child," his father murmured. "We are such lousy parents." Evelina was sniffing. Her head was nestled under her father's arms. She felt like the worst daughter in the world, making her parents feel this way. Her mother approached her from the opposite side and caressed her head.

"Since you were a youngster, you have always done whatever you wanted. Even if we attempt to stop you, you always get your way, and you are always delighted afterwards. You never regretted it," her father said.

"I don't know how we forgot it this time," Her mother said, "Maybe because we believed our daughter had matured much. Even if you had, you are and always will be our daughter." Evelina cried in her parents' arms.

She felt really privileged to have them as parents. They calmed her down, and Evelina expressed appreciation through her sniffles.

They brought Cedric back into the parlour, and he became concerned when he saw Evelina weeping. But she was safely ensconced in her parents' love, and Cedric refrained from taking her away.

"Lord Silvershire," her mother began, "I'm sorry to announce that we can't accept you as our son-in-law yet. There has only been bad blood between us."

"But we will accept you when we can pass everything down to our daughter," her father stated haughtily as he exited the parlour beside his wife. After leaving the pair together, Cedric cradled Evelina in his arms. She gazed up at him with teary red eyes.

"You better make that bloody bill a law."

The End.

In the Arms of a Rake Series

Author Note

Thank you for reading my 5th book. This standalone novel is Book 2 of 3. I would appreciate your honest opinion about the book in a review/suggestion for me to read.

Making my novels more appreciable to you is my top priority.

Thank you.

In the Arms of a Rake Series

About the Author

Emily Higgs is a vibrant voice in the realm of fiction, weaving intricate tales that transport readers to captivating worlds. With a pen dipped in imagination and a mind brimming with creativity, she effortlessly spins narratives that enthrall and enchant.

Born with a passion for storytelling, Emily's journey as a writer began at a young age when she would pen short stories and poems, each one a glimpse into her boundless imagination. As she grew, so did her love for the written word, and she soon found herself immersed in the art of crafting novels.

Her characters are equally compelling, each one imbued with their own hopes, fears, and desires. From the reluctant hero embarking on a perilous quest to the enigmatic stranger hiding a dark secret, Emily's protagonists leap off the page, their journeys leaving an indelible mark on the reader's psyche.

Printed in Great Britain
by Amazon